THE
STORYTELLER'S
DAUGHTER

Cameron Dokey

SCHOLASTIC INC.

New York Toronto London Auckland Sydney
Mexico City New Delhi Hong Kong Buenos Aires

THIS BOOK IS FOR:

❖

Lisa, always and forever the fairest of them all
Jodi, who's no slouch either
Sina, may all your storytelling dreams come true
And for Maju and her daughters

ISBN 0-439-52130-0

12 11 10 9 8 7 6 5 4 3   3 4 5 6 7 8/0

Printed in the U.S.A.   01

First Scholastic printing, February 2003
Designed by Debra Sfetsios
The text of this book was set in Adobe Jenson.

❧ Table of Contents ❧

❖Prologue❖

IF YOU WOULD KNOW

A story is alive, as you and I are.

It is rounded by muscle and sinew. Rushed with blood. Layered with skin, both rough and smooth. At its core lies soft marrow of hard, white bone. A story beats with the heart of every person who has ever strained ears to listen. On the breath of the storyteller, it soars. Until its images and deeds become so real you can see them in the air, shimmering like oases on the horizon line.

A story can fly like a bee, so straight and swift you catch only the hum of its passing. Or move so slowly it seems motionless, curled in upon itself like a snake in the sun. It can vanish like smoke before the wind. Linger like perfume in the nose. Change with every telling, yet always remain the same.

I am a storyteller, like my mother before me and hers before her. These things I know.

Yet, in spite of all this, I have told no story for almost more years than I care to remember. Perhaps that is why I have the need to tell one now.

Not just any story. My story. The tale of a girl named Shahrazad.

You sit up a little straighter in your chair. "But wait!" I hear you cry. "I have no need to hear, to read, this story. I have heard it many times before."

And this may be true, I must admit. For my story is not a new one. It is old, even as I am now old.

Though you cannot see me (not quite yet, for you have not yet truly decided to enter the life of this story), I smile. I take no offense at your objection. I can be patient, as anyone who knows even the smallest portion of my tale must know.

I watch, as your hand hovers in midair above the page. Will you go forward, or back? Turn the page, or close the cover?

There is a pause.

Then from across the space that separates us, I see the change come over you. Your hand, so still and steady just a moment ago, now trembles in a slight movement toward the next page. . . .

I smile again, for I know that you are mine now.

Or, to be more precise, you are the story's.

For I recognize the thing that has happened: You have felt the tantalizing brush of surprise. And, close upon its heels, so swift nothing on earth could have prevented its coming, anticipation.

This tale, which you thought so long asleep as to be incapable of offering anything new, has given an unexpected stretch, reached out, and caught you in its arms. Even as your mind thought to refuse, your heart reached back, already surrendering to the story's ancient spell.

Can you see me now? Not as I am, but as I was?

A young woman of seventeen years. Straight and slim, my

hair and eyes as black as the ebony wood chest that was the only possession my mother brought with her when she married my father. My skin, the color of rich, sweet honey. Others who have told my tale have said that I was beautiful. But I can see with no eyes but my own, and so I am no judge.

Are you ready to hear my greatest secret? The one that I have never spoken? You know only a small part of my story. What I am about to relate has never before been told.

I see you set the book down into your lap with a thunk. "But how can this be?" you ask. All have heard of the story-teller so gifted with words that she told tales for one thousand and one nights in a row. With her gift, her voice alone, she saved her own life and that of countless others. Through the years, this story has been handed down, with never a hint at anything left out. How, then, can what I claim be true? How can there be anything more?

Listen now. Listen truly. Fall under my storyteller's spell. Did I not say that a story could change in the telling yet remain the same in its innermost soul?

Did you truly believe that what you had been told was all there was to know?

Did you ever stop to wonder how the spirit of a man, once a wise and benevolent king, could so lose its way as to plan to make a maiden a bride at night and take her life the very next morning? Did you ever wonder how such a spirit, gone so far astray, could find its way into the light once more?

Was it truly done with words alone?

Or could it be that there was something more?

Something kept long hidden. Held back, untold. A story within a story. Not just the trunk and limbs, which have been told countless times, but something new. Something only I can tell you.

Forget all that you think you know about me. Remember that what you have heard was always told by others. You have never heard me tell my own tale before. No one has, for I have never told it. I will tell it to you now.

Listen to my name as I send it across the years. Do you not hear its power? The way the very syllables are hard and soft all at once, even as I was? They illuminate and darken. Reveal and conceal.

Whisper it now, and my story begins.

Shahrazad. Shahrazad. Shahrazad.

❖One❖

HOW THE STORY BEGINS

*O*nce, in days so long past even the graybeards among you remember them only in stories, there lived a king who had two sons. Their names were Shahrayar and Shazaman.

Now, this king was a wise man. Where other rulers raised up their sons in jealousy and anger, keeping themselves strong by causing those around them to be weak, this king strengthened himself by making those around him strong. He raised up his sons in harmony and love. And so, at his passing, his kingdom reaped not the whirlwind, but a great reward. For the princes did not quarrel over their father's earthly goods. Instead, Shahrayar, the eldest, said to his brother, Shazaman, "Hear my words, O Shazaman! You are my brother, and I love you well. Though I am oldest and could, by law, rule all, instead I will make a different choice. Hear now what I propose:

"The kingdom of our father is a vast one. Let us then divide it between us, each attending to his own domains and never making war upon the other. In this way, our people will know peace and all will prosper."

To which Shazaman replied, "Firstborn of our father, my brother, Shahrayar! Truly you are our father's worthy successor for, even in your greatness, you seek to do me honor. And, as I love you no less than you love me, I will therefore be satisfied with the lands you grant me and never seek to overthrow you."

Then Shahrayar divided the kingdom, keeping for himself the vast lands of India and Indochina. But to his brother he gave the city of Samarkand, the trade routes and the lands thereof—all jewels of great value.

And so the brothers embraced each other and parted.

But all this is yet to come, for I have let the story run on ahead of itself.

Now, at his father's death, Shahrayar inherited not only the king's lands. He also inherited his court and palace. He inherited courtiers and advisors. Chief among them, most high and highly prized, was his vizier. A fitting title! One which means, "the one who bears burdens."

What burdens this vizier was to bear in the service of his young king shall soon be told.

The vizier was older than his new master, being more of Shahrayar's father's age, and he had two daughters. Though they were far apart in years, they were close in love. The younger was a child of ten as this tale opens. Her name was Dinarzad. The elder was a young woman of seventeen. She was called Shahrazad.

Dinarzad's mother had been a great lady at court. But Shahrazad's mother had come from afar. Ah! Many were the tales told about her: Maju the Storyteller.

As a young man the vizier had led the forces of Shahrayar's father to a great victory, deep in the heart of India. When he returned home, he brought with him a bride, daughter of a people both fierce and proud. They lived not in cities and settlements as others did, but traveled always from place to place, as if their true home in the world had yet to be found. They obeyed the laws of all the lands they passed through, yet made alliances with none.

Greatly honored among them were the *drabardi*— the tellers of stories and fortunes. It was whispered that the vizier's young wife was greater than all the *drabardi* who had come before her. So great was her gift that her people wept and cast themselves upon the ground when they understood that she meant to part from them. For, once gone, she would become a stranger and could never return. So said their customs. And it had been prophesied at Maju's birth that in her time, she would come to bear the greatest *drabardi* of them all.

Though she loved the vizier, when the time for parting with her people came, Maju wept also. For many days and nights the tears fell from her eyes without ceasing, across all the miles to her new country. Only when the outrunners declared that the towers of the king's palace were actually in view did Maju dry her eyes. For the sake of a story she herself would never tell, she knew that she must put away her sorrow.

And so it was that Maju the Storyteller came to her new home. She was possessed of an intellect as sharp as the blade of a newly honed knife, and a beauty so terrible only a few could bear to look upon it. But Maju herself had never had to pass the test of gazing upon her own features. For she was as it was whispered all the truly great *drabardi* are:

Maju the Storyteller was blind.

The vizier and Maju lived quietly in their quarters in the king's great palace. In the second year of their marriage, Maju presented the vizier with a child. A daughter. They gave to her the name of Shahrazad.

Though Shahrazad grew to young womanhood in the palace, she kept herself far from the pomp and circumstance of court functions. Her father, the vizier, sat at the king's right hand. He was loved and trusted. But, even as the years went by and Shahrazad's mother showed herself to be true and virtuous, few of the people she had come to live among gave their love to Maju the Storyteller. She had not been born in that place, and the fear of such a one proved to be too strong.

And so even as the parents in the kingdom withheld their love and trust from the mother, so did they teach their children to do the same to her child. And though she never saw them nor lived amongst them,

Shahrazad grew up like the people of her mother. Searching yet never finding her true place in the world. And she grew up lonely.

The palace of the king was vast and lovely, and in it there flowed many beautiful fountains. One in particular, the young Shahrazad loved. It was not large, rather a small pool shaded by a pomegranate tree and tucked into a corner of a secluded garden. In it swam many beautiful goldfish. It was tiled with stone of such a piercing blue that looking down into the water was exactly the same as looking up into the sky.

This quiet corner of the palace was Shahrazad's favorite place—the closest she had ever come to finding where she belonged. And so it happened that one day at the beginning of her eighth year, her happiness at being in the place she loved best made Shahrazad set aside her usual caution, and she was taken by surprise.

A group of courtiers' children set upon her, lifted her up, and threw her into the pool with such force that the branches of the pomegranate tree shook above her. Shahrazad struck her head upon the stones that lined the pool and her red blood flowed out into the water.

When the courtiers' children saw what they had done, they became afraid. How terrible, they feared, would be the revenge of Maju the Storyteller! And so they fled, leaving Shahrazad sitting in a pool of bloody water, sobbing as though her heart would break. And thus her mother found her.

"Why do they treat me so?" Shahrazad cried when she saw her mother. "I do nothing to them. Nothing!"

Though she thought perhaps her own heart would break when she heard the pain and despair in her daughter's voice, Maju the Storyteller answered calmly, "Nothing is all you need do, Shahrazad, my daughter. Being yourself is enough. For you are not the same as they are, and they can neither forgive nor forget it. Come now, dry your eyes and get out of the water."

But Shahrazad was hurt and angry, and she felt rebellious. She stayed right where she was. "But I want to be the same!" she cried. "Why must I be different?" She splashed the water with an angry fist. "I won't get out until you tell me."

Before Shahrazad knew what her mother intended, Maju the Storyteller strode to the fountain, lifted her skirts, and waded into the water. She tore one of her sleeves and made a bandage to bind Shahrazad's bleeding head. How Maju knew to do this when she could not see the injury, Shahrazad did not know.

"Get up, go into our apartments, and put on dry clothing," Maju commanded her daughter. "Then go to my chest and bring me the length of cloth you will find inside."

Though her spirit still felt bruised, Shahrazad did as her mother commanded, for she understood that this was the only way Maju would give her an answer—with a story.

While Shahrazad changed into dry clothes, Maju the Storyteller stood in the water, her blind eyes cast downward. As if she could see the pool Shahrazad loved so well, now bloody and sullied. And from her eyes there fell two tears, one each from the left eye and the right. As Maju's tears struck the water, the pool was cleansed, and the water ran clear once more.

When Shahrazad returned, she found her mother sitting beside the fountain, her skirts already dry. At the sound of her daughter's footsteps, Maju held out a hand.

"What have you brought me?" she inquired.

Shahrazad reached out and placed a length of cloth into her mother's hand. It was silk as fine and sheer as gossamer, the same color blue as the stones that lined the fountain. Shahrazad watched as Maju brushed her fingers across the surface of the cloth, and she felt the hair rise on her arms.

For she knew that woven into the cloth so finely that only the hands of the storyteller could discover it, there was a tale waiting to be told. And she knew that this was the true storyteller's art. Not the speaking aloud, for that was something anyone might do, but the deciphering of the tale woven into the cloth. A secret known only to the *drabardi*.

"Ah!" Maju said when she was finished. "You have chosen well, my little one."

Shahrazad made a sound that might have been a laugh and plopped down beside her mother on the edge of the fountain.

"It was hardly a choice," she said. "That was the only piece of cloth in the whole trunk."

"That's as it should be," Maju replied with a smile. "For it means that this story is yours. Will you hear it?"

"I will," said Shahrazad.

"Then I will give you its name," said her mother. "It is called . . ."

❖ Two ❖

THE TALE OF THE GIRL WHO
WISHED TO BE WHAT SHE WAS NOT

"Once," Maju the Storyteller murmured as her fingers whispered across the silk, "there lived a girl who was very unhappy, for it seemed to her that no one loved her for what she was.

"Though she was the child of a king—a princess—she was not prized. For in a land that valued beauty above all other attributes, she was not beautiful. In a land where only men could rule, she was not a son. And so it seemed to her that although others looked upon her all day, they never saw her worth. Instead, they saw only their own disappointment.

"Yet there was one place in the palace of her father where the girl was happy. That was a small pool set beneath a pomegranate tree in the corner of a secluded garden."

At this, Shahraze day, whenad stirred, but the voice of Maju the Storyteller never faltered.

"She would sit beside it all day, watching the goldfish glide along the bottom. One day, when she was feeling particularly sad, the girl spoke her thoughts aloud:

"'Oh, lovely fish!' She sighed. 'How I wish that I were one of you! For then I would have a place in the world, and I would be admired, for all who look upon you exclaim over your loveliness.'

"Now, the princess was young, and so she did not know that it is not always wise to speak your innermost thoughts aloud. For you never know who might be listening. On this day, just as the princess was bemoaning her fate, a *djinn* was passing by. No sooner did he hear the princess's words than he swooped down and appeared to her in the garden.

"At the sight of a *djinn* suddenly materializing out of thin air, the princess was understandably alarmed. She leaped to her feet, prepared to flee. But the *djinn* spoke, and at his words, she halted.

"'Do not fear me, princess,' said the *djinn*. 'For, I have the power to grant the first wish of your heart.'

"'Tell me what it is then,' said the princess. For she knew that *djinns* did not always deal fairly with mortals.

"'That is simple,' the *djinn* replied. 'You wish to be a goldfish in that pool of water—a thing which is easily done. But because you are a princess, I will do more. I will grant you two wishes instead of merely one. The first will transform you, as you desire.'

"The heart of the princess had begun to beat so hard she feared her chest would split wide open before she could speak.

"'And the second?'

"'Will return you to your true form once more.

You have only to say the word and all shall be as I have spoken.'

"'What is the word?' asked the princess.

"The *djinn* pronounced a word of great magic. The princess repeated it, savoring the way the strange syllables rolled across her tongue. In the next instant her voice had ceased, for she was a girl no longer, but a beautiful goldfish swimming in the water.

"The *djinn* stared down at her for a moment. 'Lovely princess, I cannot leave you yet,' he murmured. 'For I would see how this wish spins out.' So he made himself invisible and hid himself in the branches of the pomegranate tree. Though a *djinn* is many things, he is curious, above all else.

"Several days went by. No one seemed to notice that the princess was missing. The *djinn* kept watch over the fish in the pool from the branches of the pomegranate tree. He thought that he had done his work well, for the princess was the loveliest color gold of all.

"On the fourth day following the princess's transformation, the *djinn's* vigilance had its reward. As he watched, invisible, from the branches of the tree, two courtiers appeared at opposite ends of the secluded garden. Ah! When they saw each other, great were their exclamations of pleasure and false surprise!

"One, who was no less than a prince—the king's designated heir and cousin to the princess—gestured the other over to the pool. He seated himself at the water's edge, trailing his fingers in the water. Thinking he might have food, the goldfish gathered around. But the young prince had no thought to feed anything other than his own ambition.

"'All is in readiness?' he inquired, being careful to keep his voice low.

"His companion nodded.'All is as you have commanded, Highness,' he replied.'Tomorrow, when you walk here in the early morning with the king, I will be hidden in the branches of this tree, which stretches out above the pool. At your signal, I will fall upon him and hold his head beneath the water until he moves no more.'

"'Then I will be king,' the young prince said.'And you shall have your reward.'

"And so the conspirators embraced each other and departed.

"Now, when the princess heard this plan, she was greatly alarmed. For, though the *djinn's* magic word had transformed her outward shape to that of a fish, she was still a girl in her heart and mind. A young girl who loved her father. The princess swam round and round the pool, trying to think of a way to warn him.

"Should she speak the magic word now? If she did, she would be herself again. She could go to her father at once. But what if he refused to see her? For the bitter truth was that the king did not often have time for his daughter. Of all those who saw the princess only for what she was not, her father was chief among them. Had he even noticed she was gone?

16

"No, the princess thought. She would wait until the morrow. The moment before the conspirators prepared to strike, she would speak the magic word, be restored to her true form, and warn her father. He would have no choice but to believe her then. She would prove her worth at last, and her father would see how much she loved him.

"And so the princess passed a troubled night and waited for the morning.

"Early the next day, just at dawn, there came a rustle of garments as the first conspirator crept into the garden. He climbed the branches of the pomegranate tree, hiding himself among the leaves. The princess bided her time.

"Soon she heard the murmur of low voices as her father and her cousin entered the garden. Still, the princess did nothing. She waited as her father approached the pond, gazing down into its still water.

"*Now!* the princess thought. She tried to speak the magic word that would bring about the transformation. To her horror, she discovered she could not! For she had no tongue to speak the word. Goldfish do not speak as young girls do. And the princess was just a goldfish, swimming in a pond.

"Desperate now, she sought a way, any way, to save her father. In a frenzy, she swam around the pool.

"'Mercy!' exclaimed the king. 'What ails the fish this morning?' In the next instant he drew back in alarm. For he had seen a face not his own, and not the prince's, reflected from above in the water. It could only be that someone was hiding in the pomegranate tree. Someone who wished to do him harm.

"When the prince saw the king draw back, he betrayed his true weak nature. He panicked in fear lest all should be lost. And so he also revealed his treachery. From his sash, he drew forth his knife.

"'Traitor!' cried the king as the young man set upon him. The prince was young and strong, but he proved no match for the fury of his uncle. They fought bitterly, and the king's robe was torn. But at last the king knocked the knife from his nephew's hand and swept his feet from under him, sending him splashing into the water. The prince struck his head upon the stones that lined the pool. His head slipped beneath the water and did not rise.

"But the king's danger had not passed. Seeing the young prince dispatched, the prince's fellow conspirator decided to risk all. With a great cry, he sprang from the tree, his knife pointed at the king's unprotected back. But before he could strike home, the fish that had first attracted the king's attention leaped from the water. Up, up, up it sailed, in a perfect arc of gold. The conspirator's knife pierced it clean through.

"The would-be assassin fell into the pond, as had the prince before him. There, he met the fate he had planned for another. For the king held his head beneath the water until he moved no more. But the fish fell to the stones of the garden, mortally wounded, and, as it did, the princess was returned to her true form.

"The sight of his daughter, her heart's blood seeping out onto the cobblestones, gave the king a greater shock than any assassin's knife.

"'My daughter! What magic is this?' he cried.

"But by then, the princess was beyond speech. She had given up her life. And so it was the *djinn* who answered for her. Making himself visible, he appeared before the king and replied, 'O King, it is mine. I heard your daughter, grieving by the side of this pool, and offered her the first wish of her heart. She thought her wish was to be a goldfish in this pool. But what the heart of your daughter truly wished above all else was that she might have value in your eyes. She has paid for this wish in the manner you see.

"'And so tell me, O King. What value do you place upon your daughter now?'

"So speaking, the *djinn* bowed before the king and departed.

"Great was the king's sorrow when he heard the *djinn's* words. For, too late, he recognized his daughter's true value. She had loved him so much she had given up her life for him, while others thought only of his possessions and would have taken his life from him.

"The king had the princess's body laid to rest with all the pomp and ceremony he could command, and declared an entire year of mourning. In her honor, he erected a statue in the pool she had loved so well.

"A fish, its eyes the blue of lapis lazuli. Each and every scale a piece of beaten gold. And from its mouth poured water as clear and sparkling as diamonds. Such was her value, for such had been the strength and purity of her love."

Maju's fingers stopped their movement among the silk. "Well, Shahrazad," she said. "What do you make of this story?"

Shahrazad stayed silent. "Never trust the word of a *djinn?*" she asked after a moment.

Maju chuckled. "Sound advice," she replied. "Your mind is quick, as always. And your heart? What does it say?"

Shahrazad sighed and put her head upon her mother's shoulder. "That I should know my own value and never seek to be what I am not."

The storyteller reached to stroke her daughter's hair. "Well spoken," she said softly. "Your heart is a strong one, my Shahrazad. With a heart such as yours, many wishes are granted, even those that seem impossible. Remember well what I have spoken."

"I will, Mother," promised Shahrazad. She felt her mother's fingers whisper along her hair. Could Maju read her the way she read the cloth? Shahrazad wondered. She lifted up her head and felt her mother's touch drop away.

"I will always be different, won't I?"

"You will always be different," Maju replied.

"And they will never like me."

"I cannot say what another will or will not do. No one can," answered the storyteller.

Abruptly Shahrazad got to her feet, her expression set. "Then I will learn to live without them."

Maju tipped her face up, as if she could really see her daughter's determined face as it stood over her.

"Do you think that such a thing is possible?"

Shahrazad snorted and turned away. "I don't know yet. When I do, I'll tell you."

At Shahrazad's sharp reply, Maju made a *tsk*ing sound with the tip of her tongue. She got to her feet in her turn, and the piece of silk she had been holding fell from her lap and floated down into the water. It settled on the surface for no more than a moment.

But in that moment, those with eyes to truly see would have beheld an image they had not noticed before. A fish, outlined in intricate stitches of shimmering gold. Then the silk sank beneath the surface of the water like sugar melting into coffee, and this fish became as any other fish in any other pond.

"I am not so sure I like your story, Maju," Shahrazad informed her as she turned to take her mother by the arm. "That *djinn* tricked the princess in more ways than one. She only got two wishes. Everyone knows you always get three."

"O, bah!" Maju exclaimed. "I waste my talent on you. Such things happen only in fairy stories. Have I not always said so?"

Shahrazad was laughing as they left the garden.

For many moments after their departure, the garden stayed still and silent. Then, there came an agitation high in the pomegranate tree, as if its branches had caught a sudden wind and held it. A face appeared amid the leaves. A youth several years older than Shahrazad shimmied down the trunk and dropped to the ground. Without hesitation, he moved to the pool, and caring nothing for his fine robes, he thrust his arms into the water, all the way to the bottom.

Although he searched until he was wet from head to foot, he could find no trace of the cloth the storyteller had left behind. Finally he simply sat beside the pool, staring down at the fish moving lazily in the water and tried to count them.

This youth's name was Shahrayar.

❧ Three ❧

SORROW

𝒩ot long after what I have just related, a great sorrow came to Shahrazad and her father. Maju the Storyteller fell sick of a fever that would not abate. No healer's potion would make the fever fall. For many days she lay upon her sickbed never moving, never speaking, with her blind eyes closed. Then, one day, she summoned all her strength, opened her eyes for one last time, and called her daughter to her bedside.

Shahrazad came at her mother's bidding. She sat beside her for many hours. In those hours Maju told her daughter many things, and Shahrazad came to understand much that had been painful and troubling. But what passed between them, what Maju spoke and what Shahrazad answered, Shahrazad would keep to herself for many years to come.

Toward evening, Maju closed her eyes once more. At this, Shahrazad left the chamber, carrying in her arms the ebony chest that had been the only possession her mother had brought with her when she married her father. No sooner had Shahrazad reached her own chambers and placed the chest beneath the window than Maju the Storyteller took one long breath and released it slowly. And with that, she died.

The moment her mother breathed her last, Shahrazad collapsed upon the floor. For many days she lay as Maju had, without moving, without speaking, her eyes closed fast. The vizier was truly in despair, for it seemed to him that the fever that had claimed the wife he loved would now also steal away his daughter. He left his apartments only to attend the king. All other hours he'd spend at Shahrazad's bedside.

But it was not until the vizier had almost given up hope that his long vigil at last had its reward. For Shahrazad's limbs stirred, and thus she spoke: "Be comforted, my father. For I am still alive and will remain so."

But when she opened her eyes, the vizier learned a bitter thing. Though his daughter lived, she had not escaped the fever unscathed. She was blind, like her mother before her. From that day forward the vizier beheld a change in his daughter. Though her love for him remained constant, Shahrazad now made good the boast she had made to Maju beside the fountain: She never left the vizier's quarters, never received visitors. Instead, she schooled herself in how to live alone.

Also from that time forward the tales about her began to spread. Throughout the land it was whispered that Shahrazad was as her mother Maju before her had been. A *drabardi*. A storyteller. And those who had been with the vizier when he had first taken

Maju to wife remembered the prophecy of her people: that Maju's child would come in time to be the greatest storyteller of all.

Shahrazad and her father mourned Maju the Storyteller for a year and a day. At the end of this time, though their hearts were still heavy, they put aside their mourning robes. That very same day, as if he had only been waiting for the moment, the king, Shahrayar's father, called his vizier before him.

"Old friend," he said. "You have served me well. Now, I desire to serve you well also. I will give to you a beautiful wife to ease your grief, for the time has come to put an end to sorrow."

Now, the vizier had no desire for a beautiful wife. He had no desire for another wife of any kind. For, save for the love he had for Shahrazad, he had buried his heart with Maju the Storyteller. But the vizier had not served the king for so many years without learning his ways. He knew a command when he heard one. And so he bowed his head and said, "My lord, you do me too much honor."

"Nonsense," said the king. And he brought forth the bride that he had chosen. She was a great court lady, as beautiful as the morning. He married her to the vizier that very hour. And so, though he had set out alone for his audience with the king, when the vizier returned to his quarters he brought with him a bride.

Now, the vizier's new wife was proud and ambitious. Never had she doubted her own value or her beauty, for all her life others had told her of it. She had not loved Maju the Storyteller, and she had no wish to love her daughter.

"Do you not think she would be happier among her mother's people?" she asked the vizier on their wedding night. "Why should she wish to stay here, among foreigners?"

The vizier looked his new wife up and down. That was all he needed to take her measure, though he was careful not to let her know it took so little time.

"She is my daughter also," he replied. "My people are hers, and her place is at my side. I will hear no more talk of sending her away."

So the vizier's new wife had no choice but to bide her time. But she had a plan, and she was sure it was a sound one. She spoke no more to the vizier of sending his daughter away. Instead, thus she spoke to Shahrazad: "Wait till I have given your father a son. I will have done something not even the great Maju could, and then we shall see how soon a storyteller's daughter is forgotten."

Though the words were designed to cut deep, Shahrazad bowed low her head and made no reply. She was still a child and had fears as all children do, but she had no fear that she might lose her father's love.

At last the day came that the vizier's new wife had hoped for: the day she could announce she was with child. Though her stepmother did not intend it

26

should be so, this news was pleasing to Shahrazad. For it meant the vizier's wife spent all her time making arrangements for the birth and no longer had time to pick and poke at Shahrazad. The months went by, and in due course, the time arrived for the coming of the child.

For many hours the vizier's wife labored to bring forth the son she so desired. But when at last the child was born, it was not a son. It was a daughter. When the vizier's wife was informed of this, she flew into a rage so great that her heart burst, and she died.

And so it was Shahrazad's arms that first sheltered her sister from the world. And it was she who named her Dinarzad.

The vizier and his daughters lived together quietly and joyfully. Though Dinarzad sometimes accompanied her father outside their quarters as she grew, Shahrazad did not. She kept true to her vow and always stayed within her own household. Many hours did she spend with nothing for company save her own thoughts and the contents of Maju's ebony trunk.

As the years went by, the vizier and his daughters grew in affection, as did the king and his two sons. The vizier's first act upon returning from his duties each day was to retire to Shahrazad's suite of rooms. There, he would tell her all that had befallen him. In this way did Shahrazad learn what transpired in her own land. Her father also placed a special set of servants always at Shahrazad's disposal. At any hour of the day or night, they might read to her on any subject she desired. In this way did she learn about the wide world around her.

The cleverness of her mind and the depth of her beauty grew with each passing year. And, as these things grew, so did the curiosity of the king's courtiers. Their earlier animosity toward Shahrazad's mother was all but forgotten, and they longed to see the storyteller's daughter. And the greatest longing of all lived in the breast of the young prince, Shahrayar, though he kept it locked away inside himself and spoke of it to no one.

But Shahrazad still kept to her own rooms and satisfied only her own curiosity.

When Shahrazad was sixteen, another sorrow befell her and her father. For in that year, the old king died and the whole kingdom was plunged into mourning. At the end of this period, Shahrayar ascended to the throne. He divided the kingdom with his brother, Shazaman, as has already been told you. The brothers embraced. Then Shazaman took his servants and his goods and departed for the city of Samarkand. And so a year went by.

Then, on no less important a day than the anniversary of their father's death, Shahrayar conceived a great desire to see his brother. He had missed him dearly for they had never been parted until now. Therefore, he sent for the vizier and commanded him to make the journey to Samarkand and bring Shazaman to his side.

The vizier made preparations without delay. He mustered a great caravan. On the day it was to depart, the streets of the city thronged with people, all loudly proclaiming their good wishes to the vizier, and their love for King Shahrayar. The king himself stood on the palace steps to wish his vizier godspeed. Dinarzad stood with the young queen and her ladies, waving a silk handkerchief in farewell. But of Shahrazad, there was no sign.

The vizier's caravan traveled for many days. When it reached Samarkand, Shazaman gave the vizier a warm welcome. When he learned the reason for the journey, he was overjoyed at the prospect of being reunited with his brother. Because the city was full of traders, Shazaman bade the vizier make camp outside the city gates. Then he set about making preparations for his own departure. It took several days, but at last the evening came when he kissed his wife farewell, and she presented him with a skin of his favorite wine.

"Tonight as you sit in your tent, drink this, and think of me," she said. "It will ease the sorrow of this parting."

"My beloved," Shazaman answered, "gladly will I do as you desire."

Then Shazaman went to the caravan of the vizier. There, he would spend the night so that they could depart early the next day in the cool of the morning.

But late that night, as he sat in his tent, a cup of the wine she had given him in his hands, Shazaman's thoughts circled back to his wife. Much as he longed to see his brother again, Shazaman's heart was sad, for he and his wife were newly married and he loved her dearly. Deciding he did not wish to part without one more sweet farewell, Shazaman set down the wine untouched, rose from his couch, and made his way back to the palace.

When Shazaman reached his chambers, his wife was nowhere to be found! Great was his dismay and alarm! He had just opened his mouth to give a cry when he heard the barest thread of sound. This was enough for him to recognize his wife's voice, so great was his love. Wary now, for he feared that something was amiss, Shazaman followed the sound. Soon he found himself on a balcony overlooking his wife's favorite garden. In the light of the moon he saw her—wrapped in another man's arms.

"What a fool is this Shazaman," he heard his wife proclaim. "For I have played him false before he has even departed. But he will never know it, for the wine I gave him at our parting is poisoned."

When Shazaman heard these words his blood ran cold as newly melted snow. The love he felt for his wife fled from his heart, never to return.

At Shazaman's wife's words, her lover pulled back. "By the love of God!" he cried. "What have you done?"

But Shazaman's wife merely laughed, a sound like tinkling bells which, as though the feeling belonged to another life or another man, Shazaman remembered had once greatly charmed him.

"Calm yourself, my beloved," spoke his wife to her lover. "For the poison is as a thief in the night. So cunningly made that no one will be able to detect its coming and going. Now let us go in and repose ourselves, for we must be ready to rule in Samarkand on the morrow."

So saying, Shazaman's wife and her lover prepared to go in. But before they could, a great rage swept Shazaman. He drew his sword and leaped down into the garden. With the first stroke, he severed his wife's lover's head from his body. The second stroke deprived his wife of her head as well. Thus did he dispatch those who would have destroyed him.

After these deeds were done Shazaman summoned his most trusted councilors and made known to them all that had taken place. They pronounced his actions true and just. Though they begged him to remain within the city lest there be other conspirators, Shazaman would not delay his visit to his brother. For he discovered that he had no wish to remain in Samarkand where everything he looked upon reminded him of the treachery of the woman he had loved.

And so, as silently as he had left it, Shazaman returned to the caravan and departed with the vizier the following morning without ever revealing to the vizier what had transpired. They traveled together for many miles until at last they reached Shahrayar's palace. Ah! How joyful was the reunion of the brothers!

But it did not take long for Shahrayar to realize that a profound melancholy had settled upon his brother. Though he would converse on any topic Shahrayar wished, Shazaman neither laughed nor smiled. Nothing seemed to delight him. But when Shahrayar pressed to know what was wrong, his brother begged him to change the subject.

In this manner many weeks went by until the time drew near for Shazaman's departure. Still trying to shake his brother from his melancholy, Shahrayar arranged a great hunt, a thing that Shazaman had always enjoyed above all others. But when the time came for the hunt to begin, Shazaman begged his brother to go without him. No words Shahrayar could say altered his brother's decision to stay behind, and so at last, he obeyed Shazaman's wishes and set forth without him.

Now, since the night he had discovered his wife's treachery, Shazaman had not slept. For it was in the night that he had discovered there was more to his life than his eyes had been able to perceive, and so he feared to close them.

And so, on a night much like the one on which Shazaman had uncovered the plot aimed at his own heart, he discovered one aimed at his brother's. For Shahrayar's wife, too, did conspire against him, to deprive him of his life and set another in his place—both in his bed and on his throne.

Shazaman was filled with anger when he heard his brother's wife plotting against him, yet his heart

was also strangely filled with joy. For now he understood that it was not he, alone, who could be
deceived. All men could be blinded by their faith in
the women they loved. Thus reasoned Shazaman.
And so he cast off his melancholy and waited for his
brother's return. But he kept a close eye on
Shahrayar's wife and her lover.

Great was the rejoicing in the city at the king's
safe return! And great was the change Shahrayar
beheld in his brother. Before, Shazaman's countenance had been dull and downcast. Now it shone so
brightly it dazzled all who looked upon him. At din-
ner that evening as they sat at their ease, Shahrayar
said to his brother, "When I departed, you were as
the ray of a lamp shielded by a hand—Shuttered and
shrouded. Now, no brightness can outshine you.
What has brought about so great a transformation? I
pray you, tell me."

At Shahrayar's words, Shazaman's expression
dimmed. "Ask me anything but that, my brother. For
my answer will bring you a grief as great as that
which I have lately known—a thing I cannot wish
upon you. Therefore, let us find another topic."

But Shahrayar was not to be dissuaded. Over and
over he urged his brother to unburden his heart. And
so at last, Shazaman related all that had lately befallen
him: How he discovered the treachery of his wife,
and what he had done about it. Great was
Shahrayar's sympathy when he heard his brother's
story.

"Now I understand your unhappiness!" he cried. "But this story does not explain why you have lately set aside your grief. Surely some other tale must follow."

"It does," replied Shazaman. "I know you have the ears to hear it, but have you the stomach and the heart, Shahrayar?"

"As we are both the sons of our father, I do," Shahrayar answered steadily, though the truth was that he was beginning to feel alarmed.

"Then hear me, and grieve also," said Shazaman. At that, he related what he had lately overheard concerning Shahrayar's own wife. How she, too, had taken a lover, and how she plotted to kill her husband and set her paramour upon his throne.

When Shahrayar heard this, he was filled with a grief and anger such as he had never known. But even in his extremity, he strove to be fair, for thus did he honor the teachings of his father.

"All that you have spoken I believe, for you have always been true to me," he told Shazaman. "Yet before I can condemn these conspirators, I must hear their guilt from their own mouths."

"That is easily arranged," Shazaman replied. "I will convey you to the place where they meet. I have kept watch over them each night, for they have yet to reveal how they intend to do you harm. But I warn you, guard well your heart, Shahrayar. There may be more pain to you in this than I have yet spoken."

"I thank you for your care," said Shahrayar. Then

the brothers embraced and went to conceal themselves.

When Shahrayar saw the place to which his brother conveyed him, he felt the first swift inklings of the pain of which Shazaman had warned. For Shahrayar himself had caused the courtyard to be built as proof of the great trust he had in his wife. None could walk there, save by her consent—not even Shahrayar.

"Come," Shazaman murmured to his brother. "Let us conceal ourselves behind that vine."

And so they hid themselves behind a vine whose sweet white flowers made the night so heavy with their scent that the very air was as a perfumed cloud. Yet it seemed to Shahrayar that the scent was bitter in his nostrils. Rank and putrid as dead meat. It was not long before the queen and her lover arrived.

How they enjoyed each other (which Shahrayar could not help but see), what words of affection they murmured (which Shahrayar could not help but hear), it is not seemly for me to tell. But I can say that when he beheld the man with whom his wife betrayed him, no warning Shazaman could have given would have prevented the pain that then pierced Shahrayar's heart.

For here was one he had known since childhood, second only to his brother in Shahrayar's love. When at last the vizier joined Shahrayar's father in the kingdom of heaven, this was the man whom Shahrayar would have promoted above all others and placed at his right hand. There was no one he had loved or trusted more, save for Shazaman.

How many minutes he stood stricken, his senses muddled with rage and pain, Shahrayar never counted. But when at last he was himself again, he saw that, from a pocket stitched into the lining of her cloak, his wife had brought forth a dagger. Ancient symbols were etched upon its blade, and in its pommel was set a ruby red as heart's blood.

At the sight of it, so great a fury shook Shahrayar that the vine around him trembled, and many of its flowers showered to the ground. Shazaman seized his brother by the arm to hold him still. But the queen and her lover never noticed, so intent were they upon themselves.

"See what I have brought you!" said the queen. "It is my husband's parting gift to his brother. At my urging, he will present it to him at a great banquet the evening before Shazaman departs. But I will drug Shazaman's food so that he sleeps like one dead. Then, in the night, we will steal this dagger and use it to slay Shahrayar."

When he heard these words, the queen's lover rejoiced and took her into his arms.

"Your mind, as always, is most excellent in its cunning, my beloved. For by this device we will rid ourselves of both these brothers. When his blade is found in the king's body, all will believe that Shazaman has slain Shahrayar. Then will we seize Shazaman and put him to death. And then there will be an end to waiting, for all that was theirs will become ours."

"Not in this lifetime," said Shahrayar. And so saying, he stepped out from behind the vine. At the sight of the friend he had so betrayed, the queen's lover fell to his knees.

"My gracious lord, forgive me!" he cried. "See how I have been bewitched! But now that I behold you here before me, I regain my senses once more. Tell me how I may serve you and it shall be done!"

"Be silent, fool!" Shahrayar's wife hissed. "Do not humble yourself so before him. Rather let us be bold and make an end of things here and now."

So saying, she raised the dagger high. But before she could strike, Shazaman stepped from his place of concealment and wrested the dagger from her, knocking her to the ground. Then with one swift stroke, Shazaman stabbed the queen's lover through his traitor's heart. His blood ran freely, forming a great pool around him. The queen knelt before her husband, her lover's blood staining her fine robes.

"Two choices lie before you," Shahrayar said as he looked upon her, and his voice was both stern and cold. "You may die by my hand, or by your own."

But the queen was defiant, even in defeat. "Give me the dagger," she commanded Shazaman. "I shall die by my hand and no other." At a nod from his brother, Shazaman placed the dagger in the queen's hand. Then she rose and faced Shahrayar.

"My trials may end tonight, but yours are just

beginning, husband. For now you know that even the most deadly of desires may be concealed in the heart you trust the most.

"Until you have found a woman whose heart you can see truly and therefore know it—one who can do the same with yours—you will find no peace by day or by night. Think well on these words, and remember me when I am gone."

So saying, she put an end to her life.

And thus began the trials of King Shahrayar.

❖ Four ❖

HOW SHAHRAZAD IS BOLD

*Y*ou shift a little in your chair, making yourself more comfortable. But what, you ask yourself, of Shahrazad? Is this not supposed to be her story? Yet she has been absent for many pages now. Surely it is time to see her again.

Patience. Though you have not seen her, she has not been idle, nor has she been forgotten. She has merely been waiting for the proper place to re-enter the story. If you look carefully, you can even see it approaching.

For many days following the death of his queen and her lover, Shahrayar behaved as always. So truly did he appear as he had always been that not even Shazaman, who loved him dearly and knew him well, could discover that there was anything wrong. So the time of Shazaman's visit drew to an end, and he departed for Samarkand once more.

But, at his brother's leaving, a change came over Shahrayar. He shut himself in the highest tower of the palace. For many days and nights, he did not come down. The sun rose and set, and rose and set again, and still Shahrayar did not come down. Some nights, the lamps burned in the tower from dusk till dawn. On still others, great bolts of lightning shot from sky to tower, and from tower to sky. And finally there came a series of nights where no lights shone forth. All within the tower was as still as death. And those were the most terrible nights of all.

Great was the fear Shahrayar's people had for him. It was whispered that he was dabbling in black magic, consulting strange and mystical signs. But when at last Shahrayar came down from the tower, the people knew a new fear—and this fear was for themselves.

For the king was as a stranger. Never had they looked upon his like before. The fact that in outward form and body he still resembled Shahrayar meant nothing. For his heart had altered so irretrievably that none could recognize it. And in this way . . . it had been turned to stone.

For all the days and nights he remained in the tower, Shahrayar had grappled with his wife's final words. They had been as a curse upon him, eating away like a cancer in his soul. For after so great and unexpected a betrayal, Shahrayar could find no way to believe it was possible to find a woman who would see his heart truly and so come to know it, yet be unafraid to have her own heart seen and known.

For even though she had deceived him in all else, in this Shahrayar perceived that his wife had spoken truly: Treachery could hide where it was least expected, even in the heart of the one he loved and trusted most.

And, so, at the last, Shahrayar could find but one

solution: He determined to set love and trust aside. In this way only could he be secure. And so he cast them from his heart. And as he did, he felt a pain so great that for many days and nights he lay senseless, as if dead, upon the tower floor. Then the day came when Shahrayar awoke and found the pain had left him. Now he felt nothing at all. He had become as the stones beneath him: Hard. Unyielding. Cold.

So he rose from the floor, and descended from the tower, and set about ruling his kingdom once more.

And now, at last, we come to Shahrazad.

Shahrayar's first act upon descending from the tower was to send for the vizier. He stayed locked in chambers with him for many hours. At the end of this time, the vizier went forth and issued a proclamation in the king's name. Copies were made and sent throughout the kingdom so that, even in the farthest reaches of his land, Shahrayar's will might be known.

Now, I have told you that the vizier had served both Shahrayar and Shahrayar's father before him. The days of the vizier's youth were long over, yet never had he seemed old. His mind and body were still strong and vigorous. But as he stood upon the great steps of the palace, the vizier's hand shook as it held the king's proclamation. And those who heard him noted that his voice trembled as he read it aloud.

"Hear now the word of your king," the vizier proclaimed. "Dire plots have been laid against him, as you all know. He could forswear the company of women forever. But, as he is both king and man, it is right and fitting that he have a wife. Learn, then, how your king will marry and yet shield himself from harm.

"Once a month, at the full of the moon, will King Shahrayar take a maiden for a wife. But, lest she plot against him as one before her has, she will be his wife for one night only. On the morning following the wedding night, she will lose her life. This course will King Shahrayar follow each month for as long as his reign lasts, save for this thing only:

"If a maiden will come forward to wed him of her own free will, she alone will know the direst consequence. All those who follow her will be only close confined. They may keep their lives, but give up the outside world forever.

"All this shall be as I have proclaimed, for it is the will of King Shahrayar."

With this, the vizier finished speaking, rolled up the proclamation bearing the great seal of the king, and vanished back inside the walls of the palace. No sooner had he done so than the love Shahrayar's people bore him began to turn to hate. For who among them would wish such a fate upon one of their daughters? How could they honor a king who exacted such a terrible price upon his subjects? The span of time it had taken the vizier to proclaim Shahrayar's will: That was how long it took for his people to turn against him and his once well-ordered kingdom to begin a descent into chaos.

As the days to the full moon drew to a close and no maiden came forward, despair spread throughout the land like a thick and choking fog. People retreated inside their homes and barred their doors, even to those they loved the most. The camels of the great trade caravans became so cranky they refused to travel. Commerce and trade came to a halt—even in far away Samarkand. Shazaman sent an urgent message to his brother, urging him to bend his will to another course and set aside what now he must surely acknowledge as madness.

Shahrayar climbed his tower, tore the message into a thousand pieces, and scattered it like leaves from the tower walls.

Finally, the night before the full moon arrived. On that night, Shahrazad left her apartments, made her way to the rooms of her father, prostrated herself before him and said, "I would beg a boon of you, my father."

Glad for the distraction, the vizier turned from his balcony where he had been watching the moon on its journey through the sky. Never had he known his daughter to ask an unreasonable thing. The truth was, she rarely asked for anything at all. So he crossed the room without hesitation, raised her to her feet, and answered, "Whatever your heart desires that I may grant is yours, my Shahrazad."

"Do you swear this will be so even before you hear it?" asked Shahrazad.

Though she could not see it, the vizier cocked an eyebrow. Rarely was his eldest daughter so forceful. It was young Dinarzad, still a child, who made demands.

"I do so swear," he told her.

"Then, hear me, Father," said Shahrazad. "First know that above all things else, I love and honor you. What I shall ask of you will be a difficult thing for you to bear. The boon I would have is that you present me to the king as his bride-to-be tomorrow. I ask this of my own free will, and you must grant it, for so you did swear."

Now, when the vizier heard his daughter's request, great was his horror! Never in his wildest dreams would he have believed that Shahrazad would ask such a thing.

"Have you taken leave of your senses?!" he exclaimed. "Think what you ask!"

"My father," Shahrazad answered steadily, "I have. Do you think I would ask such a thing lightly?"

The vizier began to pace around the room, his long robes swirling about him. So great was his distress that all signs of age left him, and he was as a young man once more.

"I wish you had not asked it at all! Aside from your mother's death, my greatest pain has been that my own people did not embrace you and Maju in their hearts. Why sacrifice yourself to save them now?"

Shahrazad tilted her head to one side, listening

until she heard her father's pacing footsteps bring him once more near her. Then she reached out and seized him by the arm.

"Be still, Father," she said. "And be comforted. For this task, while it seems hopeless, is the one for which I was born."

All of a sudden the vizier's agitation left him. Once more, he felt old. Older than when he had seen Maju lowered into her grave. Older even than when he had read King Shahrayar's proclamation to the people and seen fear replace love in their eyes.

"How can this be?" he asked. "I do not understand you, Shahrazad."

Shahrazad heard the pain and weariness in her father's voice. Her heart was struck with sorrow, though she did not let it weaken her resolve. She slipped her hand into the crook of his arm.

"Come, Father," she said. "Guide me to a seat and then sit down beside me, and I will tell you of my last hours with Maju the Storyteller, whom we both loved."

So the vizier did as Shahrazad asked, and Shahrazad revealed to him all that Maju had told her before she died.

"Do you not remember, my father, that it was foretold at her own birth that Maju would come to bear the greatest of all the *drabardi*, the storytellers?"

"I remember," answered the vizier.

"I am Maju's only child," Shahrazad continued. "Therefore, I must be that storyteller."

"How many stories can you tell," her father interrupted swiftly, "if you die the day after tomorrow?"

He thought his argument was good. But to his amazement, Shahrazad simply smiled and said, "Come now, Father, where is your faith in me?"

"It is not a matter of my faith in you, but in Shahrayar," the vizier replied. "I have searched for that faith for many days now, but, alas, I can find it no longer. I fear that it is gone."

"Then it is fortunate that I look with different eyes than yours," said Shahrazad. "Though they are blind, my eyes see things no other eyes can, for that is the true skill of the *drabardi*."

"So your mother always told me," admitted the vizier. "But what will you hope to see when you turn your eyes on Shahrayar?"

"That which must be seen, or all is lost—his heart."

At his daughter's words, the vizier rose abruptly. "Since the queen's betrayal and his sojourn in the tower, Shahrayar's heart is made of such stuff as I can hardly bear to think upon."

"Yet someone must," said Shahrazad. "For it is not merely Shahrayar, but also his kingdom which is sick at heart. Who is to say what will befall us all if the king's heart goes unknown?"

"But it is he who should know it, as all men must," protested the vizier.

"That is so," agreed Shahrazad. "But did not you tell me the queen, his betrayer, died claiming he would know no peace until another should see his heart and know it, and have her own heart seen and known?"

"I did," answered her father. "For so Shazaman told me."

"Then think, Father!" urged Shahrazad. "What torment such words must have wrought in Shahrayar's soul! Think what pain he must have endured to have cast from his heart the wise and just teachings of his father, whom he loved and honored above all. If Shahrayar no longer knows himself, then another must come to know him and lead him back to the place where he belongs."

"Perhaps," acknowledged the vizier reluctantly. "But I still don't see why that someone has to be you."

"Because it is for this that I was born," said Shahrazad. "At my birth, Maju told my fortune in the way of her people: By my skill as a storyteller, the heart of a great nation will be lost or won. That is why my skill must be greater than any *drabardi* who has come before me—even that of Maju herself. For of whose heart does the prophecy speak, if not of Shahrayar's?"

The vizier resumed his pacing. The fact that his daughter's words made sense brought no comfort to him. That she had kept the knowledge of her fate to herself for so many years troubled him greatly. She was so young, yet she had borne the burden of her destiny for all these years, alone.

"No!" he burst out. "I'm sorry, Shahrazad. But *my*

heart cannot allow you to do this. What does it matter if I am forsworn? I am old, and it's plain I am of no use to Shahrayar. Nothing I could say would sway him from his terrible course. I'll pack you and Dinarzad up, and we'll move far away. Others have done so. Why shouldn't I?"

"Because you know it would be wrong. No one can out-travel destiny, Father."

"Maybe not," the vizier snorted. "But to save you from throwing away your life, I can certainly try."

"So you will not grant me the boon I ask," Shahrazad asked after a short silence.

"No," her father said, his voice as full of certainty as he could make it. "I'm sorry, Shahrazad, but I will not."

"Then perhaps you will grant me a different one," suggested Shahrazad. "Will you go to my rooms, to where Maju's chest rests beneath my windows, open it, and bring me the length of cloth that you find?"

The vizier opened his mouth to deny this, too. Then he closed it. Standing perfectly still, he gazed into his daughter's dark and sightless eyes. At what he saw there, the vizier realized that even if he argued with her all night and all through the following day, even if he was still arguing as the words of the marriage ceremony were actually being spoken, Shahrazad would never be turned aside from the course that she had chosen. Her will was set. She had made up her mind.

And the vizier realized too that she was much like

her mother in this. And much like Shahrayar, also. And so the vizier came at last to the place he suddenly suspected his daughter had wished to lead him all along: He saw the truth of the way things were.

If anyone could come to know the heart of the king when even he had ceased to do so, it would be Shahrazad.

The vizier sighed. "Save your breath, my daughter," he told Shahrazad. "Though my heart is filled with misgiving, I will grant this terrible thing that you require. Tomorrow night, just as the moon rises, I will take you to Shahrayar and present you as his bride. And may God have mercy upon us all."

Shahrazad rose and threw her arms around him. "I pray that he may do so. Now, come, my father. Between now and then there is much I will make clear to you. But first I must speak with Dinarzad."

"Dinarzad!" the vizier exclaimed, surprised. "What can she do? She is just a child."

"Much, if she will do exactly as I ask," Shahrazad answered. "Walk with me, and I will tell you all."

❖Five❖

IN WHICH THE VIZIER TAKES A CHANCE

And so, at last the day came that King Shahrayar had appointed—the day when he would take a wife once more. On that day, he arose early, as was his custom. Though the truth was, there was hardly any purpose in his going to bed at all. Ever since the night his first queen had died by her own hand and, thus dying, had pronounced his doom, Shahrayar had hardly closed his eyes. The images he saw when he did so gave him no rest. No peace. In this, he was like his brother Shazaman had been before him.

For several hours Shahrayar went about his duties, as if this was simply a day like any other, trying to ignore the way his servants looked at him without looking—out of the corners of their eyes. But just as the sun reached its zenith, Shahrayar grew restless. He set his work aside. Gathering his robes around him, he roamed the halls of his great palace, paying no heed to the way courtiers scuttled swiftly out of the way. No attention to where he was going.

He passed through halls of stone as dark as midnight, and halls as white as a scorching noonday sky.

Halls as green as the limbs of cedar trees. As golden as the sand that stretched around the palace for countless miles. But Shahrayar's eyes saw none of these things, for they were focused inward on the landscape he had made within himself on the nights after his wife died.

At length, Shahrayar discovered that his ramblings had made him weary. He gazed about and found his wandering steps had taken him to a small courtyard. In one corner splashed a fountain. Drawing near, Shahrayar saw that the pool was tiled with stones so blue that looking down into the water was the same as looking up into the sky.

At the sight of this place he felt old memories burst into life within him the way flowers will appear at an oasis in springtime. So Shahrayar seated himself at the pool's edge—in the shade of a pomegranate tree that arched out above the water. He leaned back, looking up into the branches, and trailed his fingers in the pool. The water was as clear and bright as the surface of a mirror, but not once did Shahrayar look into it. For it came to him as he sat that his own face had become a thing he had no wish to look upon.

And thus it was that the vizier found him.

When the vizier saw Shahrayar seated by the pool that Shahrazad had loved, a very long time ago it seemed now, he was surprised to feel his spirit lighten. Into his heart, which all night had grieved and was even now afraid for the fate which would befall his daughter should she fail in her endeavors, he felt a small, bright surge of hope. The first hope he had known since he had read Shahrayar's proclamation and understood how far the young man he loved and honored had traveled away from his true self.

Perhaps, the vizier thought, all might yet be well. For perhaps the king and Shahrazad were bound together in ways he himself could not fathom, but could hope that his daughter might. So, with his fine kidskin slippers making no more than a whisper across the cobblestones, the vizier moved to King Shahrayar and bowed low.

For many moments, Shahrayar did not acknowledge the vizier in any way, instead continuing to sit gazing upward and trailing his fingers in the water. But at last, he withdrew his hand and dried it on his pant leg, caring nothing for the way the water stained the silk. He made a gesture for the vizier to rise.

"Well?" Shahrayar said softly.

At the sound of the king's voice, the vizier felt a shiver ripple across the surface of his skin, the way a wind will make smooth water ridge and pucker. *I am a fool to hope,* he thought. *How can there be hope when he sounds so cold?*

"My lord, I bring great news," he said, once more bowing low. "A maiden has come forward of her own free will and asks that you accept her as your bride."

At this news, Shahrayar sat up straight. "Who is she? What is her name?" he demanded brusquely.

"She did not speak her name," the vizier

answered, glad that he could do so honestly. There was no reason for Shahrayar to know that the reason the maiden hadn't spoken her name was that she had no need to—for the vizier knew it as well as his own.

"You would present me with a bride when you do not know her name?" Shahrayar asked, sarcasm dripping from his voice like honey from a knife.

The vizier knit his brow, as if in confusion, though his heart had begun to pound in fast, hard strokes. If Shahrayar learned his bride's identity too soon, all would be lost. Thus the vizier had told Shahrazad as they made their plans the night before. And so they had decided how the vizier would speak upon this matter, and on his speaking, all their hopes might rise or fall.

"What difference does her name make, sire?" the vizier asked, his tone perplexed and querulous in the manner he and Shahrazad had agreed upon. "Will not one maiden serve your purpose as well as any other?"

Shahrayar shot to his feet, the color in his face high. Though the king's expression was frightful, at the sight of it the vizier felt a surge of hope for a second time.

For until his queen's betrayal, Shahrayar had always been as true in his dealings with women as he was with men. Never viewing them as interchangeable, but seeking always to see each for herself alone. And so the vizier found the king's anger pleasing, for, in this, he seemed more like he had been before.

"You are certain she comes of her own free will?" the king demanded.

The vizier nodded. "Absolutely certain, sire. I knew you would wish to be reassured of this, and so I questioned her closely. She is under no outside compulsion. She seeks only to spare you grief, your country turmoil, and others the fate which she knows must surely befall her."

Shahrayar began to pace, his brow knit, his movements brusque and choppy.

"So," he said after a moment. "You would have me sacrifice a paragon."

Oho! the vizier thought. *So that is the way the wind will blow. I am not the one who set the terms of this harsh bargain, O my king. You did that all by yourself. If you no longer find them to your liking, do not make me your scapegoat.*

"A paragon? I cannot say, my lord," he said aloud. "To me she seemed a woman much as any other. Will you see her at the appointed hour or not?"

Again the quick color flashed into Shahrayar's face, and in that moment the vizier knew that he and Shahrazad had gambled and won.

"What I have proclaimed, that will I do," Shahrayar pronounced, and his voice was filled with angry pride.

Satisfied that in his pride and anger the king would pursue the identity of his bride no further, the vizier bowed low for a third and final time.

"Then I will bring her to you as you have proclaimed

it shall be," he said. "Tonight, as the full moon rises. By its light, you shall claim her as your bride."

That evening, in the cool of the twilight just before the moon appeared, the vizier went to his daughter's quarters. Shahrazad had dismissed her women and was attended only by her sister, Dinarzad. At the sight of her father, the young girl ran to him and threw her arms about his legs.

"Papa, tell her she must not do this!" she cried.

"My little one," the vizier said. With one hand, he stroked his youngest daughter's head. "Do you think I did not try?"

"Try again!" Dinarzad pleaded. She lifted her tearstained face to his. "Just one more time. I am afraid, Papa! So much depends on me. What if I do something wrong?"

"You will do nothing wrong if you do as Shahrazad has asked," said the vizier. "Nothing less, and nothing more. Go to your room now and wash your face. Let me speak to your sister alone."

Dinarzad did as her father asked, casting one look back at Shahrazad over her shoulder as she departed. When she was gone, the vizier moved to where Shahrazad had been standing silently all the while, dressed in her finest robes. They were white, and in them, Shahrazad seemed to shine like a candle flame against gathering darkness.

"You are still set on this course, my Shahrazad? It is not too late. You can still change your mind."

"I have not changed it, my father," Shahrazad replied. "Indeed, I think that I could not, even if that were what I truly wished. I cannot go back. Therefore, I must go forward."

To herself alone she kept the thought that it had been too late to change her mind in this from the moment she was born.

The vizier regarded his daughter steadily. At what he saw in her face, though his heart still grieved, his mind was satisfied.

"Come then," he said. "Say one last farewell to your sister. Repeat your instructions and ease her mind. Then I will go forward as you have told me I must: I will take you to King Shahrayar."

❧ Six ❧

THE KING TAKES A WIFE BUT
RECEIVES A SURPRISE

Just as the full moon began to climb in the sky, the vizier strode through the palace, Shahrazad at his side. The vizier was attired in cloth of silver. In one hand, he held the great curved staff, which was his badge of office. Through halls as dark as midnight, the vizier and his daughter walked together. And halls as white as a scorching noonday sky. Halls as green as the limbs of cedar trees, and as golden as the sand that stretched around the palace for countless miles.

Each place they passed was thronged with people, all longing to catch a glimpse of the woman who had come forward to be King Shahrayar's bride. But in this they were disappointed, for Shahrazad had drawn a veil across her face to avoid all chance that anyone might realize who she was.

At length the vizier and his daughter reached their destination: Shahrayar's great audience hall. Here the stones were clear as river water. Great columns of porphyry as purple-red as the flesh of plums flanked the entrance. Guards clothed all in white and armed with gleaming scimitars stood motionless on either side.

Three times the vizier struck his staff of office upon the stones to announce his presence. On the third strike, the king's chamberlain stepped before the vizier and Shahrazad, placing his body between the newcomers and the king and making himself a shield, for he was charged with keeping the life of the king secure, even if it cost him his own.

"Who seeks an audience with King Shahrayar?" he demanded.

And the vizier answered, "She who would be his bride."

At this, a sound filled Shahrazad's ears, a sound like bees buzzing in their hive.

"Does she come of her own free will?" the chamberlain inquired. "Let her answer with her own voice. By the king's command, in this, no other can speak for her."

And Shahrazad answered, "By my will and no other's."

Now the sound that came to her ears was like wind moving across the sands—a long, low sigh.

"Enter and be welcome," the chamberlain said. And he stepped aside. Together, Shahrazad and her father entered the audience hall, for the doorway was so vast they could move through it the same way they had arrived before it: side by side.

Down the length of the audience hall, the vizier and Shahrazad paced, over a floor as smooth as glass. A vast domed roof sprang up over their heads, so cleverly made that if you looked up, there were places where you could see the sky. Already the first of the evening stars were shining through it. Smooth gray columns stood straight and tall as trees along the chamber's sides. Between them, packed as tightly as salted fish in a barrel, were the members of Shahrayar's court.

The air was heavy with the scent of incense, of the agitated breath of courtiers, and something Shahrazad could not quite identify. *Anticipation,* she thought. *And perhaps fear, also.* Though the room was filled with people and the day had been warm, the air burned with cold as it struck Shahrazad's nostrils.

And so, for the first time since she had known in her heart what she must do, Shahrazad felt its steady, constant beating stumble. For it seemed to her that the cold could have its source in just one place—and that place was the heart of King Shahrayar, who soon would be her husband.

At her side, Shahrazad felt her father's footsteps slow. She slowed her own to match his, then stopped at the exact same moment he stopped. And thus it was that Shahrazad knew that her destiny was now at hand, for she had come at last to stand before King Shahrayar.

He was seated on a raised dais upon a throne of cedar, polished until it gleamed as red as an ember. On his fingers flashed rich jewels. His body was adorned in cloth of gold. As he stared down upon the vizier and the woman who stood beside him, his eyes glittered as bright as newly struck coins.

As the king's gaze moved over him, for the first and only time that he could remember, the vizier discovered he was glad that Shahrazad was blind. For he had never seen a man's eyes look as Shahrayar's did—empty of all emotion save a fierce determination to continue on the path that he had chosen. But this determination burned not hot, but with a hard and icy cold.

"You are welcome, my lord vizier," Shahrayar said, and at the sound of it, Shahrazad felt her stomach muscles clench, for never had she heard a voice so empty of emotion.

What will I do, she wondered suddenly, *if the truth of things is even worse than I supposed?*

What if it wasn't that Shahrayar's heart had been turned to stone as all had whispered? What if the king no longer had a heart at all? To see a thing that wasn't there was beyond even Shahrazad's skill.

And then it came to her that she already knew the answer to her question: If King Shahrayar's heart had left him entirely, then in the morning she would die.

"Who is this that you have brought before us?" the king asked.

And the vizier answered, "One who would be your bride. This is the hour you did appoint for a maiden to come forward and offer herself, if she would. As you proclaimed it must happen, so it has come to pass."

"Then let me see her face and know her name," commanded Shahrayar.

At these words, Shahrazad felt her father tremble, he whom she knew had never trembled in his life till now. And her father's fear helped to steady her, though Shahrazad was surprised by the knowledge that this could be so.

I have not come to die, she thought. *But to do what must be done.*

And so, before the vizier could reach for the veil that concealed her features, Shahrazad grasped it and threw it back over her head herself. Up it flew, like a bird taking wing, then settled upon her shoulders as softly as a butterfly. But Shahrazad's voice was strong as iron as she proclaimed her name.

"I am Shahrazad, daughter of Nur al-Din Hasan, the king's vizier, and Maju, called the Storyteller."

And in this way did King Shahrayar and all he had assembled within his great hall learn who had come forward to be his bride.

Absolute silence filled the audience hall. Even the courtiers were too stunned to gossip. It was a terrible silence—one that stretched on and on. Until Shahrazad lost track of how long she stood facing the king, her face bare, her body motionless, with her father quivering at her side like a horse before a race. The longer the silence stretched, the colder the air in the audience hall became, until it seemed to Shahrazad she was wrapped in the cold hand of death himself.

"What trick is this, Nur al-Din?" Shahrayar

demanded finally, in a voice both strained and harsh. "Do you think to thwart me? Do you hope, because she is yours, that I will turn aside from what I have proclaimed and, though I wed her, not require that she die tomorrow morning?"

"There is no trick," the vizier answered, and Shahrazad felt her father's trembling cease as he replied. As if the king's anger had steadied him the way his own fear had steadied her. "Nor is there any hidden design. My daughter came to me and asked for a boon. I swore to grant it before I knew what it was that she desired. If I could have found a way to deny her, believe me, I would have done it."

Then, to her surprise for they had not discussed it, Shahrazad felt her father step forward.

"Hear now what I shall proclaim, sire," the vizier said, his words coming hard and fast, as if a great dam had burst inside him.

"The moment my eldest daughter breathes her last is the moment I serve you no longer. I will take the daughter who remains to me and leave this land to travel far and wide. Everywhere I go I will proclaim to all who will listen the cruelty of King Shahrayar. And I will proclaim that your land could have no greater gift than that your heart should beat no more.

"If I had not my younger daughter in my care, I would cut your heart out and feed it to the wild dogs of the desert myself."

At the vizier's words, a sound like a flock of panicked

birds rose from the courtiers. Shahrayar rose to his feet and the sound cut off.

"Be careful what you say, old man," he warned. "To plot the death of a king is treason, and it is your life, not mine, which will be lost."

"Then so be it," the vizier answered. For he found that not even the love he bore to Dinarzad could still his tongue now that he had begun.

"Take my life if you will, but I will not take back what I have spoken. All here know that I have served you well, King Shahrayar, as I served your father before you. And always by speaking the truth. I have done nothing more than speak it to you now. If you have not the ears to—"

"I pray you, Father, peace!" interrupted Shahrazad, as she stepped to the vizier's side. "Truth or no, to speak so now does nothing but pour oil upon a fire. No will but my own has brought me to this place. This you know, for this I have spoken. Let this fact content you now, and King Shahrayar also."

There was a second pause.

"Your daughter speaks wisely, Nur al-Din," Shahrayar observed after a moment. "For her sake, I will set aside my anger and forget your rash words. But guard your tongue well, remember your younger daughter, and do not expect me to show such mercy a second time."

"Mercy is a thing I have ceased to expect from you, sire," the vizier answered.

"Enough!" cried Shahrayar. "Bring forth the holy

man, and let there be an end to talking."

At a signal from the chamberlain, the holy man who was to perform the marriage ceremony stepped forward. The chamberlain himself took Shahrazad by the hand, guided her up the steps, and placed her hand in that of Shahrayar. And it seemed to her that the grip of his fingers felt as tight and cold as prison bars.

And so it was that King Shahrayar and Lady Shahrazad were wed. With the full moon shining down upon them like a plate of silver polished by the vigorous hand of God.

❧Seven❧

IN WHICH HIDDEN THINGS BEGIN TO REVEAL THEMSELVES

Then finally, the moment came when Shahrayar and Shahrazad were left alone.

The ceremony was over, the courtiers dismissed. Last to say farewell to the new queen had been Nur al-Din Hasan, the vizier, her father. She would not see him again until the morning. If she had been successful, he would embrace her with joy when the sun arose, for she would live—if only for one day longer. If not, father and daughter would embrace in sorrow. Then, the vizier would perform his final duty for King Shahrayar and lead his own daughter to the executioner's block.

But which outcome it was to be had yet to be decided, though Shahrayar knew it not.

"I bid you welcome to my—our—quarters," Shahrayar said as he held aside a tapestry and ushered Shahrazad inside. For these rooms would, indeed, be hers, if only for this night. Gently, Shahrayar seated Shahrazad upon a low divan, then roamed the room, unable to settle, certainly unable to sit at her side. Shahrazad could hear his agitated footsteps moving back and forth.

What sort of sign is this? she wondered. At this very moment, what was going through her husband's mind?

God help me, Shahrayar thought as he prowled the room like a caged tiger. *Why doesn't she say something?*

For it had come to him suddenly as he beheld Shahrazad sitting in his own rooms that, although his will had carried him this far, it would carry him no farther. Even his imagination seemed to have deserted him, for he could conjure up nothing beyond the present moment.

What on earth am I supposed to do now?

Hardly aware of what he was doing, Shahrayar reached up to tug at the neck of his golden robes. When had they grown so uncomfortable? he wondered. For the fine cloth felt like sand against his skin, rubbing until he was raw and smarting. The collar felt like hands around his throat trying to choke him. Above it, Shahrayar's face felt brittle, as if made of cold, thin glass. He half feared to speak, lest his features should splinter and slide right off.

What is the matter with me? he thought. He had done nothing but carry out his own will. Match his footsteps to the path that he had chosen. The only one he had been able to see. Since he had first come down from the tower, it was the path that had steadied and guided him. He was sure it was the right one.

Why, then, did he suddenly seem to have lost his way? Why did everything that once seemed so right, now suddenly seem to be so wrong?

"Will you eat?" he asked abruptly. The thought of food made his stomach turn, but anything would be better than to continue dwelling on his own thoughts. Turning toward Shahrazad, Shahrayar gestured to a series of small tables near the divan. They were loaded with every kind of delicacy the palace cooks could prepare, as if they had wished the new queen's last meal to be a particularly fine one.

"Please, choose whatever you like."

At his words, Shahrazad shifted position ever so slightly, turning her body toward the sound of his voice. Shahrayar scrubbed his hands across his face. *Fool! Idiot! Imbecile!* he chastised himself. *How will she choose when she cannot see?*

How could he have forgotten that Shahrazad was blind? But there was something about her that encouraged him to forget, so sure did she seem of herself. And thus it was, so wound up was Shahrayar with his own inner turmoil, he failed to see the turmoil in Shahrazad.

He saw the pallor of her skin, but not the fine sheen of perspiration upon it, like dew upon a rose. He saw the hands clasped tightly in her lap, but not the way they gripped each other till the knuckles gleamed white as mother-of-pearl beads. He saw the fineness of her garments, but not the way they quivered in time to the too-quick beating of her heart.

Cool and remote Shahrazad seemed to him. As unafraid as she was untouched. And suddenly Shahrayar was angry that she should be so unmoved while he was not. And he welcomed his anger, for it was clean and simple. Here, at last, was a feeling he recognized.

"Your pardon," he said, his voice sounding ugly even to his own ears. "With your permission, I will change my robes. You may do so also if you wish. Shall I summon a servant to attend you?"

"No, thank you, my lord," Shahrazad answered simply. "But make yourself comfortable, by all means."

At her answer, Shahrayar bit down, hard, upon his tongue. Of course she would not change, for she had brought no other garments with her. Why should she when she would die with the coming of the sun?

I must get away from here, he thought.

"For a moment, I will leave you, then," he said. Turning, he pushed aside a hanging and vanished into the depths of his apartments.

For several moments, Shahrazad sat perfectly still, her only movement her steady breathing in and out. At first this brought no peace, for with every breath she took, her mind repeated the same phrase, over and over:

What have I done? What have I done? What have I done?

And, just as swiftly as her mind posed the question, her heart gave the reply: *What I must. What I must. What I must.*

For years she had unconsciously schooled herself

to face this test, teaching herself to rely upon herself alone. Now she would be up to the task that lay before her, the one Maju had told her was her destiny, or she would not. And if not she, then no one.

But it will be hard, she thought. *Ah, God!* Much harder than she had thought. For though she had listened for it carefully, it seemed to her that she had heard no warmth in Shahrayar at all. He was cold, through and through. So cold that Shahrazad could feel it in the very marrow of her bones.

With a jerky motion she unclasped her hands, ran one of them nervously over the fabric of the divan, then paused. Slowly, more carefully now, Shahrazad explored the fabric beneath her fingers. At the unexpected feel of what she found there, she felt her thoughts steady and her courage revive.

For what she felt beneath her fingers wasn't the subtlety of silk. It was the simplicity of finely woven cotton. Here, in this place that was most truly his, Shahrayar surrounded himself not with things to compel and impress, but with things to make a refuge and a home. And the knowledge of this warmed Shahrazad's heart, as she hoped to find the way to warm Shahrayar's.

And so she sat, her fingers stroking the fabric of the divan. And thus it was that Shahrayar found her. Coming back into the room, certain now that he had himself under control, he caught the gentle motion of Shahrazad's hand and stopped short. For the first time he thought he saw Shahrazad's mother in her.

For the first time it occurred to him to wonder if, like Maju, Shahrazad could see things that others could not.

And at this wondering, Shahrayar felt something move within him, even within his heart that he, himself, had turned to stone. But what it was, he could not tell. So he continued into the room and watched the way Shahrazad heard the sound of his coming and turned her face toward him once more.

"Ah!" she said, and he saw the way her face lit up. "You are much more comfortable now."

"I am, indeed," Shahrayar answered. "But how can you tell?"

"By the sound of your movements," Shahrazad said. "You walk with more ease than you did before. And the sound of the fabric is gentle as it brushes against itself." She cocked her head, as if considering. "You are wearing a caftan, and your feet are bare, like a boy's."

"That is so," Shahrayar said, his tone astonished. At the sound of it, Shahrazad gave a laugh like chimes in the wind.

"There is no magic in this, I assure you," she said. "More like a lucky guess, my lord. My father often dressed this way when he came to see me at the end of the day after his court duties were done. He told me he had acquired the custom from the old king, your father. I simply thought you might have done so also."

At the mention of her father and his own,

Shahrayar sobered. "I have no wish to speak of fathers."

"As you desire, so it shall be." Shahrazad's smile faded away, and the room was filled with silence once more. At this, Shahrayar felt the thing inside him stir again, but this time he thought he knew its name: It was called sorrow.

"What will you have to eat?" he asked, after a moment. *And now I am back where I started*, he thought, only this time, he discovered he was hungry.

"I would like to try whatever pleases you," Shahrazad answered promptly.

Shahrayar felt his face color and was glad she could not see it. He simply did not understand the way she treated him. Where was her anger? Her resentment? Her fear? Her hate? Was she so cold and untouched that she felt none of these things?

"Why?" he inquired.

"So that I may get to know you better," Shahrazad said, as any new wife might. As if the meal she and Shahrayar were about to take was merely the first of many they would enjoy together, instead of the only one. And now the thing within Shahrayar was called pain. And as he recognized it, it burst forth.

"*Why?*" he cried again. And, though the word was the same as he had used just moments before, both he and Shahrazad knew the question he posed was not.

"For the love of God, Shahrazad! For years you have kept yourself apart, since you were nothing more than a child. Now you come forth for this. I do not understand you."

Nor I you, my lord, thought Shahrazad. *How can you travel so far from yourself and not even perceive that you are lost?*

But she spoke none of this. Instead she said, "Because it is what I wished, Shahrayar."

He gave a sharp, unbelieving laugh. "What you wished," he echoed. "Do you mean you wish to die?"

"Of course not," answered Shahrazad. "I wished—" Her throat closed suddenly, and she cleared it. She knew that she must speak the truth in this, but it was a difficult one to tell.

"I wished to be the one to truly see, to come to know your heart. At least, I wished to try."

At her words, Shahrayar felt his stone heart give a crack, and the pain surged forth into his veins, scalding as lava. *Too late. Your wish has come too late,* he thought.

"How will you see it?" he asked, his tone bitter. "How will you see anything truly? You are blind, Shahrazad."

The words hung, awful, in the air. And Shahrayar discovered he could hate himself.

"That is so," Shahrazad answered, her voice calm. "Do you think that is the most important thing about me? If eyes are all one needs to see and know another's heart truly then answer me this: When you look at me now do you see and understand *my* heart?"

Shahrayar was silent for so long, Shahrazad

feared he would not answer. But at last he replied, "No, I do not, Shahrazad."

"Then perhaps you should not be so quick to judge what I can do, though my eyes see not as yours."

"You think that I'm a monster, don't you?" Shahrayar asked, the words tumbling forth before he even knew they had been formed.

"No," Shahrazad answered swiftly. "Not that."

"What, then?" asked Shahrayar.

This time it was Shahrazad who paused before she answered, for had she not just told herself she would not speak of this? But he had asked, and so she answered truthfully.

"I think that you are . . . lost."

"Lost!" Shahrayar cried, stung. "Do you think I am a child, then?"

"No," Shahrazad answered steadily. "Only that you act like one. A great kingdom is in your hands. All look to you, yet you see only yourself, Shahrayar."

A shocked silence filled the room. Not since he had truly been a child had anyone spoken to him in this manner, Shahrayar thought.

"I am the king. How dare you speak so to me?"

"And I am the queen, if only for this night," Shahrazad answered, as her chin came up stubbornly. "What will you do to punish me for answering truthfully when you bid me speak? Kill me before my time is up?"

"Enough!" Shahrayar exclaimed, for her words

horrified him. Did she truly think him capable of such a thing? *But why not?* he answered himself. Had he not proclaimed that she would die tomorrow morning, and for even less cause?

"I have no wish to quarrel, Shahrazad."

"Nor I," said Shahrazad. Then, to Shahrayar's amazement, her mouth quirked up. "But you make it hard not to, you know."

Shahrayar gave a startled bark of laughter, all his anger suddenly gone. It felt good to be with someone who was not afraid to speak her mind, he realized to his surprise. His first queen had certainly never spoken to him so. Now that he thought about it, they had barely conversed at all. Perhaps if they had . . .

No, Shahrayar thought. He would not travel down that road. There was no sense in comparing the one who had betrayed him to Shahrazad. That much, he could already tell.

"I will make you a bargain," he said now, careful to keep his tone light. "I will admit that I am quarrelsome if you will admit that you have a sharp tongue."

His first wife would never have taken such a bargain, Shahrayar thought. She would have denied his faults, for was he not the king? And, in denying his, she had hidden her own.

"Well, of course I have a sharp tongue," Shahrazad said, as if Shahrayar had but stated the obvious. "I am the daughter of a storyteller, am I not?"

"That is so."

"Well, then," Shahrazad said, and she extended

her hand, as if to seal the bargain. Shahrayar took it between his own. For the first time, he learned how soft Shahrazad's hands were. And how warm. And he felt the way her fingers trembled within the cage of his.

"All this bargain-making has made me hungry," Shahrazad said as she slid her hand from his. "I thought you promised me food, my lord."

"So I did," Shahrayar admitted. He filled a plate, sat down at her feet, and they shared a meal in companionable silence.

But again and again as they shared the food, Shahrayar's fingers met those of Shahrazad. Until he found himself craving her touch more than the food. What it would be like to set the meal aside and simply touch her? To run his fingertips across her palm and up her arm until he had coaxed her head down upon his shoulder. What would his own head feel like resting on her heart? he wondered. Could the very beating of it have the power to warm him?

When he realized the direction his thoughts had taken, for the first time since the night he discovered that he had been betrayed, Shahrayar realized how weary and confused he was.

Shahrazad is right, he thought. *I am well and truly lost.*

And for the first time, he realized how cold he was.

But just when his thoughts would have given him over to despair, he was pulled back by the sound of Shahrazad's voice.

"Might I beg a boon of you, my lord?"

"Do I get to know what it is ahead of time?" Shahrayar asked, glad to be distracted from his thoughts. But as he turned his head to look up at her, he caught the line of worry between Shahrazad's brows, and he was sorry that he had teased her so. "You may have whatever you wish," he promised swiftly, "if the granting of it brings no stain upon my honor."

"I swear that it will not," said Shahrazad. "You know I have a sister, who is but ten years old."

Shahrayar nodded, though he felt his stomach sink. "Dinarzad."

"It has always been my custom to say good night to her each evening," Shahrazad went on. "Might she be permitted to come to me here, so that I might wish her both good night and farewell?"

"Such a thing is easily granted," Shahrayar said. But his throat felt thick, for he remembered the grief that he had felt upon his first parting with his brother, Shazaman. This parting of the sisters would be both first and last, and he himself would be the cause.

"It grows late. Do you wish to send for her now?"

"If it pleases you," said Shahrazad.

"Stop doing that!" Shahrayar burst out before he could help himself. He rose, and set their empty plate upon a nearby tray.

"Stop behaving as if you were my servant. It does not suit you, Shahrazad. I like the sharp edge of your tongue better than the dull one. I seek to please you in this. Just say what you want."

God knew, there was little enough else by which he could please her, and he had suddenly discovered that pleasing her was a thing he wanted, very much.

If Shahrazad was distressed by this outburst, she did not show it, answering merely, "Then it would please me to send for her now."

So Shahrayar clapped his hands to summon a servant to fetch Dinarzad. When she was brought, she threw herself at once into Shahrazad's arms. Her tears flowed freely, for she had yet to learn the way to conceal her feelings, being but a child. And Shahrayar was moved at her grief.

"Would you like me to leave you alone?"

At his words, Dinarzad's head shot up. "No! You must not!" she cried.

"Dinarzad, remember you are speaking to the king," Shahrazad remonstrated softly.

Dinarzad's face colored and she bit her lip. "That is . . . I beg you to stay with us, my lord. There is something I would ask of my sister, but you alone can answer yea or nay."

"What is it that you wish?" asked Shahrayar, intrigued.

"My sister tells me a story each night before I sleep," Dinarzad explained and, though her eyes managed to meet Shahrayar's without flinching, her voice was soft and small. "She reads the cloth in the way of her mother, Maju the Storyteller. For as long as I can remember, she has done this, but after tonight—"

But here her eyes filled with tears once more and she was unable to go on.

So the rumors are true, Shahrayar thought. *Shahrazad has become a storyteller, like her mother before her.*

"You would like her to tell you a story," he said. *One last story.*

Dinarzad nodded.

"By all means," said Shahrayar, pleased that he could grant her wish. At his words, Dinarzad gave a great sigh. Her distress seemed to leave her, and she nestled her head upon her sister's shoulder.

Above the young girl's head, Shahrazad's eyes met those of Shahrayar. In that moment, it did not seem to him that Shahrazad was blind. Instead he thought she saw him very well. Though what she saw when she looked at him, Shahrayar could not tell. Then Shahrazad looked down, and the moment passed.

"Thank you," Shahrazad said softly. "Will you please send for my trunk? Only then will I be able to do as my sister has asked."

And Shahrayar said, "I will do so at once."

And now it was Shahrazad who sighed, for though she knew her greatest test still lay ahead, she was satisfied that it was well begun.

❧Eight❧

DINARZAD SETS THE FUTURE IN MOTION

"Very well, little one," Shahrazad said to her sister after the trunk had been brought. "You know what to do by now. Open the trunk and hand me the length of cloth you will find inside."

But to Shahrayar's surprise, Dinarzad did not at once obey her older sister's instructions. Instead, she pulled Shahrazad's head down. Then, she whispered something Shahrayar could not hear, her dark eyes flashing to his face and then away.

"If that is what you wish," Shahrazad said, when her sister was finished.

"It is," replied Dinarzad.

"Will you ask him, or shall I?"

"You do it," Dinarzad said.

"My sister wonders whether or not you would like to choose tonight's story, my lord."

"Me?!" Shahrayar exclaimed, genuinely surprised. "But why?"

"Tell him," Shahrazad urged gently. "Don't be afraid."

"It's just—" Dinarzad faltered. "I wondered—" She pulled in a breath and plowed on. "My sister has told me many tales, one every night since I was strong enough to open Maju's trunk. But it does not hold stories just for me. It holds tales for all. Do you not wish to hear one?"

"I do wish it," said Shahrayar. And found with the saying of it that it was true.

You have raised this child up well, Shahrazad, he thought. For, like the rest of the court, he had heard the tales surrounding Dinarzad's birth. *She is generous where others would find cause to be selfish, just as you are.*

"Then, if you please, my lord," said Dinarzad, and she gestured to the trunk.

So Shahrayar knelt and opened the ebony trunk that had once belonged to Maju the Storyteller. As he did so, he heard a sigh like the final gust of a windstorm pass through Dinarzad. He glanced up to find her dark eyes regarding him solemnly. He smiled, and she smiled back. Then Shahrayar gave all his attention to the trunk.

Deep inside he thrust his hands, reaching down, down, down—a very long way it seemed to him—until his fingers touched the very bottom. Then up and down and back and forth Shahrayar swept his hands until he was certain he had covered every inch of the trunk's interior.

Nothing. There was nothing.

Ah God, I cannot bear this! he thought.

What if his true destiny was this: Always to be unable to obtain what others seemed to come by without thought.

What had Dinarzad said? That Shahrazad had

told her a tale each night since she had first grown strong enough to lift up the lid of the trunk. How many times had she reached in and pulled forth the thing she longed for, each time successful though she was just a child?

But for the king, it appeared, there would be nothing. No tale, just as there had been no trust.

No love.

No! Not this time! thought Shahrayar. *This time will be different. This, I vow.*

And as if his vow contained the power of a wish, his hands found the thing they had been searching for.

Shahrayar seized the piece of cloth in his hands as he drew it forth as if he were afraid it might escape him now that he had found it. Then almost at once, he relaxed his hold. Passing the cloth from hand to hand as if trying to learn its texture. To figure out how Shahrazad would be able to perceive and decipher what he could not.

Though the finding of it brought him wonder, to Shahrayar it still seemed but a simple piece of cloth. It was thick and heavy, its texture rough in some places and smooth in others. It seemed to cling to his hands, then slip away all in the same moment. Even its color seemed changeable, so that he could not truly say just what color it was.

"This is all that I could find," he said at last. He sat back upon his heels and raised the cloth to Shahrazad.

"That is as it should be," Shahrazad answered as

she stretched out her arms. Shahrayar laid the cloth across them. "For it means this story is yours. Will you hear it?"

"I will," said Shahrayar.

At these words, Dinarzad sighed once more. Shahrayar closed the lid of the trunk, lifted it, and set it aside. Dinarzad then curled up at her sister's feet. Shahrayar retired to a nest of cushions nearby.

For many moments Shahrazad did nothing but sit silently, her head bent, as if listening to the story within the cloth. Then she began to move her fingers from side to side across it—on one end only, Shahrayar noted. Not from end to end, as if to learn the tale in its entirety, but only the place where it would start. Though how she knew which end was which Shahrayar could not even begin to guess.

"This tale is subtle. It has many twists and turns," Shahrazad said at last. Then to Shahrayar's secret delight, she smiled. "As befits the mind of a king, perhaps."

"Perhaps," agreed Shahrayar.

"It is long, as the life of a king should be," Shahrazad went on. "Are you sure you have the will and the patience to hear it through to the end?"

"I do," Shahrayar vowed.

Though he expected her to begin at once, Shahrazad sat perfectly still for the count of a dozen heartbeats.

"Then I will give you its name and begin," she said at last. "The story you have chosen is called . . ."

❧ Nine ❧

THE TALE OF THE KING WHO THOUGHT HE COULD OUTSHINE THE STARS

"Once, in a country so far away that you and I will never visit it, there lived a king who desired one thing above all others: to have a son. He had a wife of many years whom he loved dearly, but, because she had given him only daughters, he divorced her and set her aside. He then chose a new, young wife who was beautiful and virtuous, as his first wife had been in her youth, a thing the king had conveniently forgotten.

Surely, he thought, *a wife such as this will give me the son I have desired for so long.*

"But this marriage proved more disastrous than the first. For, while the king's first wife had at least given him daughters, his second wife gave him no children at all. Finally the king decided to consult an oracle. Something in the stars was working against him. This much now seemed certain. He needed to discover what it was and what sort of sacrifice might be required of him. Not a very great one, he hoped. So he kissed his wife the queen and set off.

"For many days the king traveled, making his

journey to the oracle on foot, for so it had always been done. For all in this country knew that those who see what no one else can care nothing for the trappings that make others so proud. And so the king took no servants or retainers; he wore no fine clothes but only simple pilgrim's garments. After several days of traveling by both day and night, he reached the foot of a great mountain. Its top was shrouded in clouds. None could remember when it had last been seen. But there, all knew, stood the oracle and the seer who could read the stars.

"Now, at the foot of this hill ran a stream so clear you could see every stone in the streambed. Its water was as pure as starlight itself, and so cold that people did not drink there to slake their thirst for fear the water would freeze their throats closed. For many hours the king walked alongside this stream, searching for the place where he might cross it and find a way up the mountain. Just as the sun began to sink in the sky, he realized he had walked the entire way around the mountain's foot and arrived at the place where he had started. And still he had not found the way across the stream and up the mountain.

"Discouraged, the king sat by the streamside to rest himself while he considered what to do next. Try as he might, he could reach no other conclusion than that he would have to brave the icy water in order to reach the oracle.

"No sooner had he reached this conclusion than the king heard a rustle and a stomp behind him.

Leaping to his feet, he spun around and beheld a woman so old she was bent over nearly double. Her features were folded in upon themselves like a piece of fruit left too long in the sun. A milky-blue film covered the surface of her eyes. The king found the sight of her revolting. He was not accustomed to such ugliness.

"His first thought was to drive the old woman away. But at the last moment, the king remembered that he stood at the foot of the oracle. If ever he should be on his best behavior, this was the place. So he resisted his first impulse and spoke to the old woman kindly.

"'What do you here, Mother?' he asked. 'Do you come to consult the oracle?'

"'My business is my own and none of yours,' the old woman replied in a voice as dry and scratchy as a sandstorm.

"The king felt a spurt of anger at her words, for no one had spoken so to him in a very long time, if they ever had at all. Yet he mastered himself a second time, for now he remembered something else: It was said all were equal in the eyes of the oracle.

"'Though you will not reveal it, I will aid you in your business if I can,' he promised.

"'Excellent,' the old woman replied at once. 'Then take me upon your back, and carry me across the water.'

"When the king heard this, he was greatly dismayed. For though he had been growing accustomed to the way the old woman looked, that was hardly the same thing as being willing to touch her. Still, he knelt and took her upon his back as she had demanded, for he could see no other option. Then, binding up his robes so that they at least might stay dry, the king waded out into the water.

"It was cold. So cold it sucked the breath from his lungs and made spots dance before his eyes. A cold that made his legs burn like fire. The stones of the streambed were slick as glass beneath his feet. At any moment, the king feared that he might slip, tumble all the way into the swift-moving current, be pulled under, and drown.

"His back itched with the desire to fling the old woman from it and plunge alone toward the opposite shore. But again, the king mastered his impulse. What he had started, that he would complete. No sooner had he thought this than he felt his feet touch the far bank. Up, up, up, the king climbed. Until his head was spinning and his ears rang. Until it seemed to him that he would climb as high as the very stars themselves.

"Then suddenly the climb was over. The ground grew smooth and flat beneath his feet, covered with grass as thick and soft as a finely woven carpet. The king fell to his knees. The old woman slid from his back.

"'That was well done,' she said. 'And a deed well done should always be rewarded. Ask your question, and you shall have an answer for it.'

"With that, she cast off her tattered cloak, and with it, her very form. Before the king's astonished eyes she altered until a young woman stood before him, lovely and strong. Her long dark hair streamed down her back, black and lustrous as the night sky. Her eyes shone clear and bright and were as silver as the stars wheeling above her.

"And thus it was that the king realized that it was the seer herself whom he had carried across the water. And that what he had taken for the bank of the opposite shore had, in fact, been the mountain.

"And so he knew that he had come at last to the oracle.

"'What is it that you wish to know?' the seer asked as she seated herself upon the ground.

"'If you please,' the king said, suddenly humble, 'why is it that I have no son? It is what I have longed for above all else.'

"'Show me your hand,' the seer instructed.

"The king held it out. The seer took it between hers and studied it carefully, running her fingertips back and forth across it. At her touch, the king shivered, for it was as cold as the water he had crossed to reach this place, and her skin was as smooth as the stones on the river bottom.

"'A man may not always have what he desires, even if he is a king,' the seer observed at last, and at her words the king felt his heart clutch. 'You have many daughters. Do you not love them?'

"'Yes, but—,' the king said, then stopped short.

"'Ah!' the seer commented, when he failed to go on. 'Though you are a king, I see that you are still as many other men are. You do not see what you have, but long to see what you have not.'

"At her words, a great fear and an even greater despair seized the king. 'Is it then hopeless?'

"The seer did not immediately reply but lifted her face up to the stars. And it seemed to the king that he could see the myriad patterns of them etched across the surface of her skin as if the seer bore the mark of the very universe itself.

"'It is not hopeless,' she said at last. 'Though your way may be hard. For thus say the stars. If you see what you desire but claim it not, long will be your path and great your sorrow.'

"Though her words were solemn, when he heard her proclaim them, the king felt a great weight lift from his heart. For it seemed impossible to him that he might see his son but claim him not. His wife would give birth; a midwife would place the infant in the king's arms. In jubilation, he would hold him high for all to see and declare 'I here see and claim my son.' When one was a king, such things were simple.

"'I do not fear this prophecy,' the king spoke out, his tone bold. And he saw above his head a single silver star go streaking across the heavens.

"'Ah!' the seer exclaimed, her gaze still upon the sky. 'So you think the light of your will can outshine what is written in the stars?'

"'I am a king,' the king said proudly. 'I am not as other men are.'

"'We shall see,' the seer replied. 'Go now, for you have made your choice, and what is done cannot be undone. All that remains now is for you to play it out.'

"So saying, she vanished, leaving the king to make his way alone back down the mountainside.

"He set off swiftly, his spirits high, determined to reach his home as soon as possible. With every step he took, the king became more and more certain that when he arrived at his palace, he would be greeted by the news that his young wife was with child. This time, he was sure, it would be the son for whom he had longed for so very long.

"*Who does that seer think she is?* the king thought as he marched along. *Why should she see my destiny more clearly than I? Other men may be ruled by what the stars proclaim, but not me. I am a king and therefore not as other men are.*

"And so, by degrees, the king worked himself into a righteous fury at the way the seer had spoken to him—and worked himself out of heeding the warning of her prophecy. Thus occupied by his thoughts, he walked mile after mile, hardly noticing the passage of time. Indeed, it seemed to him that he marched through a contradiction; time either moved very, very swiftly or not at all. For even though he walked until his limbs ached and his brain grew fuzzy, neither night nor day seemed to come or go, but he moved always through a strange gray twilight.

"Finally the king began to realize a dreadful thing: Though he had walked until he was more tired than he had been in his entire life, he had not yet reached the stream that wound around the foot of the mountain. And with this realization came a great fear.

"What if, in this place of enchantment, he had become well and truly . . ."

But here, Shahrazad's voice was interrupted. Into Shahrayar's apartment came a new sound: the crowing of the first cock of the morning. Its raucous greeting of the day ended on a note that sounded exactly like triumph, and then was gone. The room was filled with silence. As if awakening from a dream, Shahrayar stirred and gazed around him.

Dinarzad was still curled up at her sister's feet, her eyes closed, her breathing deep and even. Shahrayar himself still sat upon his nest of cushions, so enthralled by Shahrazad's tale that he was in exactly the same position he had been when she first began to tell it. He hadn't so much as moved a muscle.

He had not noticed the passing of the hours. Neither the full moon setting, nor the stars snuffing out like the flames of a thousand candles, one by one. Instead he had stared up at another night's sky, in the company of another king. One he greatly feared was on his way to ignoring what was right in front of him and so was setting out upon a path that would be both long and filled with sorrow.

But with the crowing of the cock, the dream had been shattered and Shahrayar returned to the real world once more. Day was here, impossible to ignore. Now he saw the way the sky had turned soft and pink like the inside of the shell his father had brought him once following a great victory on the shores of some faraway ocean. Never had he seen so beautiful and terrible a sight, thought Shahrayar, save for one thing only: When he looked on Shahrazad. His bride. His wife. His storyteller.

By his word, she had become all these things. And by his word, her life would end with the coming of this bright morning.

❖Ten❖

SHAHRAYAR SURPRISES MANY,
BUT HIMSELF MOST OF ALL

*W*hen he realized what was to come, Shahrayar felt a great trembling in all his body, clear through to his stone heart.

No! he thought.

He did not stop to puzzle at his own swift rejection of what he had himself proclaimed must be so. He knew only one thing: Though the morning had come, Shahrazad must not be allowed to die.

I am the king, he thought. *If I can will one thing, then I can will another.* Though what this thing should be, he did not yet know. But he rose to his feet, and at the sound of this, Shahrazad spoke for the first time since she had broken off her tale.

"Is it day, then, Shahrayar?"

Shahrayar felt his throat constrict, but he answered steadily, "It is day, Shahrazad."

"Where is my trunk?" Shahrazad asked, and so surprised him. For she made no reference to what must follow the rising of the sun.

"Behind you."

"Will you take me to it?"

"Of course."

So, mindful of Dinarzad who still slept, Shahrayar took Shahrazad by the hand and led her to the trunk. She knelt before it, placed within it the piece of fabric holding the secrets of the story she had begun, then gently closed the lid and said:

"I am sorry, Shahrayar."

"What for?" he asked, the surprise plain in his voice.

Oh, what a great fool I am! thought Shahrazad. Surely it would have been better if she had not spoken. For how could she put what she was feeling into words? To do so might end her task almost as soon as it had begun.

She was not sorry to have become Shahrayar's wife. Not sorry to have taken up her tale. To her, the way that she must take seemed as clear as it always had. Her motives were true and just.

But it had come to her through the course of the long night that where she perceived a path running straight and true, Shahrayar might perceive a different one. A way so filled with twists and turns that it could never come out straight.

Might not her actions appear like deception should he learn what she had done before he had truly come to trust her? How deep might such a wound cut, having been so cruelly deceived by a wife before?

He had not spared her life—not yet. Not even for a moment longer. But if he did, surely he would believe it was the result of his own will. It would not occur to him that it could be the result of her story-teller's art, also.

If he should see what she had done through any but the eyes of love, what would befall them both?

"Shahrazad?" Shahrayar prompted.

"Never have I begun a tale I could not finish," Shahrazad answered slowly. "Perhaps I should not have given my sister her way in this. Her tales are short, for she is just a child. But you are a man full grown. I should have realized a tale that belonged to you would take more time. We may never know how the story ends, and for this, I am sorry."

At her words, Shahrayar felt something explode inside his head. *I see it now,* he thought. *The way to keep her alive.*

"I do not accept your apology," he said. He leaned down and helped Shahrazad to her feet. "For I promised I would hear this story through to its end. Therefore I will do so."

At his words, Shahrazad's heart gave a great leap, though she answered, "But—"

"Oh, do be quiet and let me think a moment," Shahrayar exclaimed as he spun away in frustration. "Why must you always ask one more question? Why can you never let things be?"

"I suppose because I cannot help it," Shahrazad said. "It is the way that I am made. What if the telling of this tale takes many nights, Shahrayar? More than you now can perceive?"

"Then it will take as many nights as it takes! I am

the king. All must abide by what I proclaim."

"So you keep saying. But will what you proclaim today still be so tomorrow?"

"How should I know?" Shahrayar all but shouted, and Dinarzad stirred and moaned in her sleep. "Do you think I have all the answers just because I am king?" he asked, his tone suddenly weary and quiet.

"No, I do not think that," Shahrazad said. "For surely a king is first a man. And so it must follow that a king does as all men do: the best he can."

At her words, all Shahrayar's anger and frustration left him for wonder. *She understands.* She did not expect him to be perfect just because he was the king, nor did she expect him to hide or deny his flaws as his first queen had.

And so he moved back to Shahrazad and took her face between his hands.

"You ask me questions for which I have no answers. They are all in the future, and I cannot see that far. I can only see this moment and it confuses me, for it contains things I did not think to find."

"Then let us solve one puzzle, at least," suggested Shahrazad. "I will tell your story each night until it is done, and rejoice in the telling of it."

Shahrayar felt her words sink, deep inside him, like water into parched ground.

"I thank you for your generosity."

At his words, Shahrazad's mouth quirked up. "Now I know you are just a man," she said. "For I think you have grown confused over which of us is the generous one."

"No, I have not," answered Shahrayar.

And he realized suddenly that the two of them were standing body to body and that he still cradled Shahrazad's face in his hands. At this, a longing to kiss her rose so sharply within him that it felt like pain. He released her and stepped back.

"Come," he said. "Let us summon a servant to carry your sister. Go to your father and tell him what has come to pass. I think he will want to hear it from you, rather than from me. I hope that it will bring him gladness."

"I am sure it will," Shahrazad said.

And at that moment, the sun appeared through the window and shone upon her face so brightly that even her blind eyes were dazzled.

❧Eleven❧

A PLOT

And now, for a moment, we must leave Shahrayar and Shahrazad. Though they are the heart of this tale, a thing that is right and fitting for it is theirs. There are others who must be spoken of, for, without them, the tale cannot travel to its proper end.

I have told you how, in the time following his discovery of his first queen's betrayal, Shahrayar locked himself in his highest tower and did not come down. Great was the fear and compassion his people had for him during these days—before he descended from the tower and all perceived that his heart had been turned to stone.

But what none perceived was that it was not Shahrayar alone whose heart was altered during this time. There were others whose hearts were changed as well. First among them were the former queen's brothers, and their hearts were transformed in this way: They were turned into pillars of flame that burned with a desire for revenge. Until it was accomplished or their lives were ended, the fire could never be put out.

Now, Shahrayar had been a prince before he had become a king, for that is the way things usually go.

And so it follows that his first bride had been a princess, daughter of a kingdom taken by Shahrayar's father in one of the many wars of conquest at which he so excelled.

The land he had conquered brought Shahrayar's father great wealth and, though he was glad he could now call it his, he did not want its people humbled too much. He wanted them to retain their pride, for they had become his people, and their pride had therefore become his.

So he married Shahrayar to the sister of the young king he had defeated. The princess was very beautiful, and this suited Shahrayar's father's plans well. For in this way, he hoped to secure both his son's happiness and the allegiance of those who had been his foes.

The prince and princess had been married two years and two days when Shahrayar's father died and Shahrayar ascended to the throne. They had been married three years and thirty days when Shahrayar stood in the garden beside his brother, Shazaman, and saw his wife embrace another. Heard them plot murder even while they murmured words of love. On that night, the marriage ended, for the queen died by her own hand, cursing Shahrayar as she did so.

When the queen's five brothers learned what she had done, at first, they were glad that she lived no more. For, by her actions, she had brought a stain upon their honor that could never be erased. But even as Shahrayar lay upon the tower floor changing the very fabric of his heart, so did the queen's brothers begin to change their hearts as well.

The eldest was the first to put his feelings into words. Disgraceful as they surely were, were not their sister's actions actually all her husband's fault? he inquired of his brothers.

King Shahrayar had allowed his wife great liberties, a thing which was not wise, as the eldest brother had cause to know, for had he not been a king himself once?

But this Shahrayar had been so foolish as to create the very garden in which his queen and her lover had plotted against him. He had even gone so far as to proclaim it a place no one, not even he, himself, could enter but by the queen's will alone. Such dealings between men and women simply were not natural.

"Our eldest brother is right," the second declared, a thing that caused the others to stare at him in wonder for none could remember the last time he had agreed with his elder brother.

These brothers were not like Shahrayar and Shazaman. They were so jealous and quarrelsome, they disagreed about everything save the rising and setting of the sun. For these things seemed so sure and set in their course that even the brothers could find in them no fault.

"Women are weak creatures," the third brother said, now picking up the refrain. "They require great guidance and careful watching."

Surely "freedom" was a word that had no place in a woman's vocabulary, he went on. In fact, her vocabulary should contain as few words as possible: Husband. Obedience. Duty. Hearth. Home. These were words a woman should learn well. If she knew these, she need know little else.

"That is so." The fourth brother nodded wisely, though he did not yet have a wife of his own. "And to that end, women should be kept indoors, within their own households." This was not cruelty, but a kindness, he reasoned, for it was better for them so. Life inside the home was the only kind of life that women understood, the only kind they were capable of understanding.

At this, the brothers clasped hands across the brazier around which they were gathered, congratulating themselves on the fact that for once in their lives, they were in accord. Why all men did not think as they did, they could not tell. But this much, they did know: If women were allowed too much liberty, either of mind or of body, trouble was bound to be the inevitable result.

And so, by these degrees did the brothers convince themselves that the deeds of their sister had, in truth, been her husband's fault. And no sooner had they convinced themselves of this, than the desire to be revenged against him—and so remove the stain upon their honor—sparked up and began to glow red-hot. For at Shahrayar's feet could be laid the true source of their shame: He had failed to govern his wife.

If a man could not govern his own wife, how could he be expected to govern a country? the brothers asked themselves. And so, at last, they convinced themselves of one final thing more: Removing Shahrayar would not simply be revenge. It would be justice, also.

And so they began to plot to remove Shahrayar and place the eldest brother upon the throne. But bringing down a king is no easy matter, as many who have tried it have discovered to their cost.

The eldest brother was all for action. "Let us raise an army and storm the palace!" he shouted, leaping to his feet.

The second brother pulled him back down with one quick yank on his arm. "Get a hold of yourself," he ordered sternly. "And keep your voice down. This we certainly shall do, but in secret and slowly. To raise an army takes money and time. Is there nothing that can be done till then?"

"What about poison?" the third brother inquired.

"Impossible," the fourth instantly scoffed. "We could never get close enough to Shahrayar. We're too well known."

"All right, then, we'll hire an assassin," the third brother countered, not yet ready to give up his idea.

But this suggestion only increased the fourth brother's scorn. "And pay him what? Have you forgotten that we've no money? Besides, paying someone else to do our dirty work is a risky business. They can always be bought again by someone else for a higher price. It's our honor that has been sullied. We should handle this ourselves."

"How?" the first brother spoke up again, glaring at the second and fourth brothers in turn. "You don't like our ideas, fine. At least we came up with something. That's more than I've heard from you two so far."

"You didn't come up with something, you came up with the most obvious thing," the second brother replied. And so the argument was off and running.

They quarreled for hours until their eyes grew scratchy with smoke from the brazier, and their voices grew hoarse. And at the end of this time, they still knew two things only: They must discover who could be found to bear arms to support them, for they could not hope to completely overcome Shahrayar on their own. In the meantime, the best way to keep an eye on him was from inside the palace. But who could be trusted to do this, they did not know. The brothers were about to retire to their separate chambers in frustration when the fifth and youngest brother spoke for the very first time.

"Let me go."

At this, his elder brothers jumped like the guilty conspirators they were, for the truth was that they had entirely forgotten the presence of their youngest brother. They often did this, for he was but a youth of fourteen years old. More than old enough to join in their councils, according to their customs. But the youngest was unlike his older brothers in almost every regard. He was quiet and studious, slim and slight of build; not sturdy, boisterous and warlike as the others had been when they were young. The truth was that they did not understand him, mistaking his quiet air for inattention at best, and cowardice at worst. What they did not understand, they had chosen to ignore.

All the while as the others had been scheming and plotting, bickering and arguing, the fifth brother had been curled up like a mouse in the room's farthest corner. He had watched, and he had listened, but he had made no sound at all. Now his voice fell upon the ears of his brothers like a plunge into icy water, shocking them speechless.

The eldest was the first to recover. He strode to where his youngest brother was now sitting up straight and raised his hand to strike him. But the second brother grabbed his arm and held it motionless.

"What are you doing?" the third brother demanded angrily of the second brother, taking the first brother's side as always. He thought striking their youngest brother was a fine idea. It was the best way to impress the need for secrecy and silence upon him.

"Wait," the fourth brother counseled, stepping between his second and third brothers. He always took the second brother's side. In this way, the brothers were always balanced in their quarrels.

"We have discussed this matter fruitlessly for hours," the fourth brother reminded the others. "It is too late to prevent him from overhearing, for he has been here all along. Therefore, let us listen to what our youngest brother has to say."

"What he has to say?" the eldest brother mocked as he yanked his arm away from the second. "What can he have to say? He is just a boy."

"Exactly," his youngest brother piped up, unimpressed and unoffended by his eldest brother's show of temper. He had big fists, it was true, but his brain was small. Had he not allowed them to be conquered?

"Who pays attention to a mere boy? Not even you, my brothers. But those whom others do not notice may still see much, and they may do even more."

At his words, a sudden silence filled the room. It was broken when the second brother laughed suddenly. He leaned down and pulled his youngest brother to his feet.

"Are you not cold in this corner, small one? Come sit by the fire and tell us what it is you think you can accomplish that we cannot."

"Just this," his youngest brother said when all were seated around the brazier once more. "I can get into the palace. Once there, I can find a way to get close to King Shahrayar."

The first and third brothers both gave barks of derisive laughter, but the second and fourth leaned closer.

"How?"

◆◆◆◆◆◆

"Many inside the palace know your faces, as you have already noted," the youngest brother said, "for they fought against you when our country was lost. But they do not know my face, for I was too young to fight. I have been inside the palace only once, on the day our sister was married to Shahrayar. Few had reason to notice me then. All eyes were on the prince and his bride."

"But you can't be sure," the eldest brother objected, more for form's sake than that he disagreed with what his youngest brother had said. There were principles and hierarchies to be maintained. Elder brothers deserved respect, not to be contradicted by those who were younger than they. "Someone may have noticed you."

"Why should they?" the youngest brother asked with a smile as sweet as a honey cake. "I am just a boy."

The second brother chuckled, causing his older brother's face to turn the color of sour wine.

"Suppose we get you a place in the palace," the third brother said. "What then? How will you accomplish what must be done?"

"I don't know yet," his youngest brother answered honestly. "How can I know ahead of time? I will keep my eyes and ears open as I always do. When the time comes, I will know, and I will seize it. I will cleanse the stain from our honor and be revenged upon King Shahrayar."

"Oh, this is nonsense!" the eldest brother exploded, leaping to his feet. "I will not trust something so important to one so young, this one least of all."

"Shut up and sit down!" the second and fourth brothers roared.

At this, all eyes turned to the third brother, the only one who had not yet indicated what he thought.

"For once, I must agree with the others," he said, a thing that caused the eldest brother's mouth to open and close like a fish out of water, for the third brother had never disagreed with him before.

"We have talked all night and come up with nothing," the third brother went on. "Perhaps a boy may accomplish what we may not. Why should he not have a chance? His dishonor is as great as ours."

And so it was decided. The very next day the second brother, whose brain was the most devious, found a way to send his youngest brother to the palace as kitchen help. It was below his station to be sure, but there was an advantage in this that could not be ignored: If others overlooked children, they overlooked servants even more. One who was both a servant and a child would therefore be all but invisible. So the second brother reasoned as he made his choice.

And so the youngest brother settled into life at the palace not long after Shahrayar came down from the tower. He was there when the vizier proclaimed Shahrayar's intent to take a wife again. He was there when the king wed Shahrazad. He even managed to have a hand in preparing the wedding feast, helping to carry it to Shahrayar's private quarters himself.

And, through it all, the youngest brother did what he did best: He watched. He waited. And he kept his eyes and ears open, never doubting that one day, his time would come.

❖Twelve❖

SHAHRAZAD IS JOYFUL, AND THE CONSPIRATORS MAKE A DISCOVERY

And so it came to pass that on the same bright morning that Shahrayar decided to spare Shahrazad's life for at least one more day, his first queen's youngest brother labored in the palace kitchens, keeping his ears open in between mopping his brow. Dinarzad was put to bed, having fallen asleep somewhere in the middle of her sister's story. And Shahrazad herself was reunited with the vizier, her father.

Their reunion was a joyful one, but it did not last long. For no sooner had Shahrazad returned to her old rooms and told her father what had come to pass than they were interrupted by a frantic pounding at the door. It was opened to reveal the chamberlain, his face bright red and his breath huffing in and out.

"My lord vizier, my lady Shahrazad—that is—I mean to say—Your Highness—," he panted.

"For heaven's sake," Nur al-Din cried out, genuinely alarmed. Never had he seen the chamberlain look like this, and he knew how important the other man's dignity was to him. Next to his love for the king, it was the thing he kept closest to his heart.

"Stop worrying about getting our titles right and get to the point."

"The king," the chamberlain gasped out. "You must go to the king at once."

He was in his private audience chamber. Not the room he used for show, the one in which he and Shahrazad were wed, but the one from which he conducted the true business of running the country. It was simply furnished. At one end, tall windows looked out over the largest of the palace courtyards.

Though she could not see it, Shahrazad knew the room well, for her father had described it to her many times. She could tell at once that the windows were open, for into the room there came a sound like the movement of the sea, a sound that both swelled and swallowed itself up all in the same moment.

"I am glad you have come, Nur al-Din," Shahrayar said as the chamberlain ushered the vizier and his daughter into the room, then, at a wave of the king's hand, bowed himself back out again. No one hearing Shahrayar would have guessed at the bitterness which had so recently passed between him and his vizier.

"Let your daughter stand back from the windows, but come here yourself, and tell me what you make of what you see."

Shahrazad's father gave her arm a quick squeeze, then moved to do the king's bidding. After a moment he said, "It is a crowd, my lord."

"I can see that for myself, thank you," Shahrayar replied, his voice sharp. "It is their purpose that I cannot fathom. The captain of the guard said they began to gather before sunrise. I had him command them to disperse, but they refused. I fear this may be an uprising."

"They do not appear to be armed," Nur al-Din observed, though he had to admit Shahrayar might have good cause to be alarmed even so. Never had he seen so large a crowd assemble in the courtyard, save for the funeral procession honoring Shahrayar's father.

"Did your captain ask them why they had come?"

"I am the king," Shahrayar said. "Would you have me inquire of my own subjects?"

"Well, it does seem to be the most straightforward way of learning their intentions," the vizier said.

"I know why they have come," Shahrazad spoke up from behind them.

She heard the scrape of Shahrayar's sandals as he turned around.

"You what?"

"I know why they have come," she said again. "And why they have refused to leave. Are these things not plain to you also?"

Shahrayar made an exasperated sound. "If they were plain to me, I would hardly have had the chamberlain summon you and your father at a dead run. Stop talking in riddles, and tell me what you think you perceive that I do not."

The vizier's head swiveled back and forth as he watched the exchange. *They speak to each other as if they have been married for years,* he thought.

"They came to see an execution," Shahrazad said simply. "And they have refused to leave because they do not understand why there has not yet been one."

There was a beat of silence. In it, though Shahrazad could hear her own breath and—she thought—her father's, it seemed to her that Shahrayar breathed not at all and that even the voices in the courtyard below had fallen silent.

"You mean they came to see *your* execution," Shahrayar said at last. "Merciful God. What kind of a king am I that my people are so bloodthirsty?"

"It may not be that," Nur al-Din put in swiftly. "My first thought when I beheld this crowd is that I had not seen so many assembled since the passing of your father. Perhaps they do not come because they think my daughter's death will be a sport, but to pay witness and to honor her. By her death, many will live."

"I think that they are afraid," said Shahrazad.

"Afraid," Shahrayar echoed, struck. "By your actions, they have been spared. What have they to fear?"

"*Your* actions, my lord. What you have proclaimed must be has not come to pass. Does this bode well or ill? You alone can tell them."

"You think I should explain myself to my own subjects," Shahrayar said.

"I think you should allay the fears of the people who loved your father, and who love you, also," replied Shahrazad. "Fear makes people unpredictable. They become like—"

"Children," Shahrayar interrupted, for now he saw which way her thoughts were going. "Their fear makes them think of themselves alone. But I am king, and I must think of all."

"It is a wise king who thinks so," agreed the vizier.

Shahrayar gave a snort. "So you agree! I should have known. Very well. I will tell my people what is in my mind, for to me this course seems right and just. But I shall not do so alone. Let us stand together upon the balcony, Shahrazad, that all may look upon you when I proclaim that you are to live as long as your story does."

"As the king commands," Shahrazad said, and she moved to take her husband's hand and stand by his side.

And Shahrayar told his people what had taken place the night before. That Shahrazad had begun to tell him a story of such wondrous deeds, he could not bear to end her life until the tale was over. For as long as her story lasted, so would her life.

Upon hearing this news, the people wept with amazement and joy. For, in showing such mercy, it seemed to them that the king they had so loved had returned to them once more. And they laid this miracle at Shahrazad's door. So they shouted all together, with one great voice, "*Long live Queen Shahrazad!*"

But even though they lifted their voices as high as the rest, the former queen's brothers looked at one another in triumph out of the corners of their eyes. For it seemed to them that Shahrayar had just put a weapon into their hands—one they had never expected to find there.

He had a weakness, and her name was Shahrazad.

❧Thirteen❧

SHAHRAZAD RESUMES HER TALE

"*Now,*" said Shahrazad that night, "where was I?"

"I know! I know!" Dinarzad cried. "You were telling about the king, and how he was well and truly . . ."

"Dinarzad," Shahrazad interrupted, laying a hand on her younger sister's head, for Dinarzad sat at her feet just as she had the night before. "Remember that this is not your story, but Shahrayar's."

At Shahrazad's words, Dinarzad caught her breath. How could she have forgotten herself so? she wondered. Her relief that her sister had been spared, her delight that Shahrazad's plan seemed to be working had driven every other thought from Dinarzad's mind. It had even made her forget her awe of Shahrayar.

I cannot afford to forget, she thought. *Not while he holds Shahrazad's life so tightly in his hands.*

She hung her head. "I beg your pardon, my lord."

"I wish you wouldn't," Shahrayar said easily from where he stood near the trunk. Never guessing what was in Dinarzad's thoughts, knowing only that he was secretly delighted that she was as interested in the story as he was. "To tell you the truth, I'm glad to know I'm not the only one who is so eager."

At his words, Dinarzad's face lit up in a surprised smile. Shahrayar smiled back. *This is how it should be,* he thought. *Comfortable. Like a family.* And suddenly his whole body was flooded with so many different sensations that he could make no sense of any of them, and he sat down upon the lid of the trunk.

"My lord!" Dinarzad cried in alarm. "Are you all right?"

"I think so," Shahrayar replied, though the truth was, he was far from certain. When had the room grown so warm? "It's just—perhaps a glass of something cool to drink?"

"Dinarzad," Shahrazad said. "Ring for a servant, and have him bring His Majesty a cup of water from the deepest well."

Dinarzad did as her sister instructed while Shahrayar sat motionless upon Maju the Storyteller's ebony trunk, a great tingling filling all his limbs, but most particularly the region of his heart. The room around him began to shimmer, and suddenly it seemed to Shahrayar that he could see his future unfurling like a great silk ribbon before him.

He blinked, for his eyes were all but blinded by the vision's textures, its richness, and its color. The life he suddenly envisioned blazed with possibilities, and the greatest one of all was the one he least expected: the possibility for love.

But as yet this chance was nothing more than a

bright glimmer in the distance. To reach it, Shahrayar perceived that he would have to pass through places where he could not see his way straight, if at all. Places where the road was filled with traps and shadows. With a thousand nameless, faceless, unguessed-at things that could deprive him of the love for which he suddenly so longed. And just the thought of these dangers twisted like knives in his heart.

For the first time, he began to understand just what he had made of himself in his high tower. For the first time he began to perceive just how terrible it would be to live a life that was truly without love. Worse than terrible—it would be impossible.

Then Shahrazad spoke, and the vision wavered and vanished.

"Here is some cool water, my lord."

Shahrayar blinked again and saw Dinarzad's concerned face bending over him. "Thank you," he said. And he took the cup and drained it in one long swallow. "Now," he went on, rising to his feet and tossing his cup to the young serving boy hovering in the background, "let us have our story."

And so saying, he knelt and opened the trunk. The cloth came to his hand as if it had been waiting for him. He took it out and brought it once more to Shahrazad. And as he placed it in her hands, he thought he heard her sigh. Shahrayar took up his same place among the cushions. Dinarzad curled at her sister's feet as she had the night before.

"Now, let me see," Shahrazad said as her fingers

roamed the cloth. "Oh, yes. The king was well and truly . . ."

Lost, Shahrayar thought.

"*Lost.* Or so he feared when he realized he had been walking for as long as he could remember, yet seemed no closer to reaching the stream at the bottom of the mountain than he was when he had left the seer and started out. And in all that time, the sun had neither risen nor set, but the king had walked through a pearl-colored twilight.

"Without warning, the words of the seer came back to haunt him. Had she not said his way would be both hard and long? So great did the king's fear become when he remembered this, he came to a complete stop, and for many moments was unable to go on.

"*Oh, get a hold of yourself,* he commanded himself finally. *Stop acting like a baby and start acting like the king you are. You can't really be lost. You're still on the mountain, after all.*

"Besides, the seer had not said that his way would be long and hard no matter what. It would be so only if he saw his desire and claimed it not. The king still considered this possibility highly unlikely.

"*Remember you are in a place of enchantment,* he reminded himself. And at this, he grew incensed at the unfairness of it all. How were mere mortals supposed to find their way when those who were more than mortal made all the rules but would not reveal what they were ahead of time?

"As a king, he could not approve of such a thing. And so, by degrees, instead of allowing his fear to make him humble and careful, the king worked himself up to a fit of righteous indignation. And because of this, he lost his caution as thoroughly as he had lost his way.

"'I want off of this mountain,' he declared. 'I don't care how.'

"Now I will share with you a thing that Maju once shared with me," Shahrazad confided to her sister and husband, her voice melodic and low. "And that is that you should always think at least twice before you speak your innermost thoughts aloud. And more than twice in a place of enchantment where things may have ears that do not in the day-to-day world.

"And if things that do not usually have ears suddenly possess them, it may be that they have mouths and tongues and wills also. And if they have these things, who knows what they can do?"

"Thus the king soon discovered when he heard a voice declare, 'Let me help you.'

"At this, the king was so startled that he lost his footing, tumbled to the ground, and began to roll. Down, down, down the mountain he went, taking quantities of earth and rocks with him as he tumbled along. Just as he was sure his very bones would be crushed within him, the miracle occurred.

"*Thump!*

"With a great crash, the king collided with something. A thing that made a grunt and a cry. He was no longer rolling, and for that the king was grateful. But he was also cross, for the thing that had stopped him was treading on his beard, which suddenly seemed much longer than the king recalled. No sooner had it ceased to tread on his beard than it pulled his hair, which brought tears to his eyes. And so, instead of speaking in gratitude, the king spoke sharply.

"'Stop that! Why don't you watch where you're going, you great oaf?'

"Now, I'm sure you will agree that this was hardly the way to speak to another person, for so this thing turned out to be. Particularly a young man whose strong and sturdy body may have just prevented yours from rolling right off the side of a mountain. But by now the king was feeling so altogether thwarted, tricked, and vexed that he no longer cared for anyone but himself, and so he no longer cared how he sounded.

"'What are you doing here?' he demanded crossly as he got to his feet and did his best to dust himself off. 'How dare you bump and bruise me? Don't you care who I am at all?'

"'Not in the least,' the young man said. 'Why should I? I am on a great quest to find my long-lost father. I was doing just fine until you came tumbling down upon me. A thing which probably saved your life, by the way. You might try being a little nicer.'

"'I most certainly will not!' roared the king. 'The least you could have done was to notice me coming and get out of the way.'

"'If I *had* noticed you, I would have,' the young man roared back, 'but you came from out of nowhere.' All of a sudden his eyes narrowed. 'Perhaps that was your intention,' he said. 'Perhaps you rolled into me on purpose to thwart me in my quest.'

"'Oh, don't be so ridiculous,' the king snapped. 'I've never met your father, and if you're the best he can do for a son, I'm not surprised that you haven't either. He probably ran away from you. All I'm trying to do is to get off this mountain.'

"At this, the young man pointed downhill. 'Try going that way,' he said.

"'I *know* that!' the king shouted. 'What do you take me for, a total idiot?'

"'No, only a rude, insensitive boor who rolls into people and then yells at them for no reason,' the young man shouted right back.

"At this, the king lost his temper so completely he did a thing which, had he been himself, would have shamed him deeply. He picked up a stone, intending to bring it crashing down upon the young man's head. But no sooner had he raised it high than to his complete and utter astonishment, the stone spoke and said, 'Your wish is my command.'

"The young man gave a yelp and jumped back. As for the king, he was so amazed, he almost dropped the stone right on his foot.

"'Did you say something?' the king asked.

"The young man gaped, his mouth wide open, his

eyes as big and round as two full moons.

"'Of course I did,' the stone replied. 'I said, your wish is my command.'

"'Wait a minute, what wish? I didn't make any wish,' the king sputtered.

"'Oh, yes, you did,' the stone said. 'I'd hold on tight, if I were you.'

"With that, the king was lifted high into the air. Up, up, up they went, until the young man was just an astonished speck on the ground below them.

"'This can't be happening!' the king gasped.

"'Don't be so ridiculous,' the stone answered in exactly the same tone of voice the king had used just a few moments earlier. 'Of course it can. How many stories have you heard about carpets flying? Carpets! Hah! Have you ever heard of anything so stupid? How anyone ever came up with that idea, I can't possibly imagine.'

"'At least if you were a carpet, I could sit down,' the king said. For, truth to tell, his arm was starting to get a little tired.

"'Oh, well,' the stone replied, its tone disgustingly cheerful. 'At least now we're on our way.'

"'On our way *where?*' the king wailed.

"'Well how on earth should I know?' the stone asked, its tone beginning to get a little testy. 'You were the one who wished to get off the mountain. You wished for it twice, in fact. You never said where you wished to end up. Don't blame me for your lack of foresight.'

"'How can these things be?' the king asked.

"'Oh that is simple enough. I am enchanted.'

"'I was afraid you were going to say that.'

"'Watch out,' the stone suddenly advised. 'Flock of birds ahead. This could get a little tricky.'

"The king closed his eyes and held on for dear life. *Oh, dear, oh dear,* he moaned to himself as he heard the flutter of wings around his head. How had such a thing come to pass? He was really just an everyday king with an everyday wish. All he wanted was a son. Was that too much to ask?

"*Squawk!*

"In sudden horror, the king opened his eyes just in time to see the last bird of the flock coming straight for him, its claws outstretched. Another moment, and it would peck his eyes out for sure. With a great cry, the king let go of the stone and covered his face with his hands.

"'I really don't think you should have done that,' he heard the stone say. But by then it was too late. As swiftly as he had risen, the king began to fall, and it seemed to him that the earth rose up to meet him at an alarming rate. Try as he might, the king could see no other outcome but that his life must end.

"'Alas, alas!' he cried aloud. 'I wish I had not died before I had the chance—'"

But here, as before, Shahrazad's voice was stilled by the crowing of the first cock of the morning. And so her tale ended, still unfinished after a second night. And Shahrayar discovered he was glad that this was so.

"Surely this king must be the most foolish man alive," he commented. "For he is so busy wishing for something that he cannot see when it is right in front of him."

"Fortunate for him, then," Shahrazad said, "that he lives only in a story."

At these words Shahrayar snorted. He took the cloth from Shahrazad and tucked it safely back inside the trunk. As he did so, Dinarzad yawned, stretched, and sat up. When she realized that it was day, she drew in a swift breath and glanced fearfully up at Shahrazad.

"Do not fear," Shahrayar spoke up. "Your sister's story is not yet ended." Dinarzad gave a sigh. "You should return to your father's quarters and sleep in your own bed, little one," the king went on. "For I fear that you are very tired, and your sister is also."

So the sisters embraced. But when Dinarzad moved toward the door, she stopped short and gave a cry. At this, the chamberlain burst in through the door, then promptly tripped over a figure sprawled just inside. For many moments, all was pandemonium. When at last order was restored, Dinarzad knelt on the floor, her arms wrapped around a serving lad not much older than she was while the chamberlain stood above them, his expression fierce and his sword drawn.

"Move aside, young mistress," he commanded.

"I will not!" cried Dinarzad. "Can you not see he is just a boy?"

"No matter," the chamberlain answered. "He is where he should not be, and must suffer the consequences."

"*Enough!*" cried Shahrayar. He moved to stand beside Dinarzad and the boy. "We will not make war on children, chamberlain. Put up your sword."

"But . . . Your Majesty . . . ," the chamberlain sputtered.

"Do as I say!" roared Shahrayar.

The chamberlain sheathed his sword. At this, Dinarzad scrambled to her feet, pulling the serving boy along with her, and sought shelter for them both in her sister's arms.

"Now then," said Shahrayar. "Let us see if we cannot get to the bottom of this great confusion." He knelt down so that he and the boy were face to face, a thing that made the chamberlain take a step forward in alarm. "Suppose you tell us who you are and what you are doing here, my boy."

Serving lad and king regarded one another for a moment. *So close*, the young boy thought. So close, yet there was nothing to be done. No way to exact the revenge for which he and his brothers longed. He had no weapon of any kind, not even a pin to poke this King Shahrayar in one inquiring eye. He had only an empty cup.

And my wits, he thought. If ever he had need to use them well, now was surely the time.

"I did but bring the water as I was commanded, my lord," he said, and he held out his empty cup.

"Ah, the water!" Shahrayar exclaimed, as he stood up. "I remember now. I did call for water. But surely that was last night. How do you come to still be here this morning?"

At this, the boy began to squirm as if confused, though, in fact, his thoughts were racing and he squirmed to buy himself some extra time. A thought had suddenly blossomed in his brain. Perhaps he had a weapon after all.

"If you please," he said, his tone obsequious. "I meant no harm. I only wanted to hear the story, to hear for myself if what they say is true or no."

"What do they say?" asked Shahrazad, speaking to him for the first time. He could feel her voice vibrate against his body, and realized he still stood protected by the circle of her arms. At this, he gave a little wriggle and she released him. He snuck a quick glance at her face as he answered, "Why, that there must be magic in it, of course."

"Magic!" exclaimed Shahrayar. "Why should that be?"

"Because the king did not do as he proclaimed, and all for the sake of a story," the boy replied. "What else but magic could make a true king go back on his own word?"

At this, the chamberlain hissed, "Silence, you impertinent ruffian."

"Leave him be," Shahrayar commanded. He took

a turn about the room, his expression thoughtful. "Tell me, my young fellow," he said at last. "May not a king simply change his mind?"

"But—," the boy said, then broke off.

"It's all right," Shahrayar said. "Go on."

"Surely a king must be strong," the boy said. "What he commands must come to pass, for his word is law. Who will respect him if he's always changing his mind?"

"But what if in changing his mind, he rights a great wrong?"

Without hesitation, the boy shook his head from side to side. "That could never happen," he said boldly. "What a king proclaims is right to begin with, or he is no true king at all."

At this, Shahrayar's eyes became opaque and expressionless. "Do you think so? I perceive that your mind is a sharp one, at any rate. Too sharp to be a ... what?"

"A kitchen boy," the lad said, and he hung his head as if in shame, though in fact it was to hide his expression of triumph. Though he had used no weapon but words, nevertheless he thought that he had struck a blow.

"What is your name?" Shahrayar asked. "Do I not know you?" There was something about the lad's face that grew in his mind the longer he looked upon him.

"I am called 'Ajib," answered the boy, but to the second question he gave no reply. For 'Ajib was his true name. He and his brothers had considered giving him a new one, but the second brother had decided against it at the last moment. It would be one more thing that might cause confusion and send their plans awry.

"Well, 'Ajib," said Shahrayar. "As of this moment, you are a kitchen boy no longer. Since you show such an aptitude for politics, I will place you in the household of my vizier so that you may learn from him whether your notions of what makes a king are true or no. Do honor to the lady Dinarzad, his daughter, for without her protection you might have come to harm."

At this, the boy turned to where Dinarzad stood beside her sister and made a bow. "I will honor both the vizier's daughters to the best of my ability," he vowed.

"Well spoken," said Shahrayar.

In this way did Shahrayar take a stranger into the bosom of his family. Though whether this would turn out well or ill, not even 'Ajib himself could know.

❧Fourteen❧

THE CALM BEFORE A STORM

And now there came a time when the days and nights flowed into one another like the great silk ribbon in Shahrayar's vision. Nights when Shahrazad spun out her tale, her voice falling silent only with the first cock crow of the morning.

Nights when the lamplight glowed softly over her hair and skin, and Shahrayar discovered he wanted no world other than the sound of her voice. Nights when the scent of jasmine wafted in through the open window and Shahrazad found herself happier than she had been since her mother died. Her mouth filled with tales, her sister and young 'Ajib curled at her feet, and her heart full of wonder for what was coming to blossom there for Shahrayar.

For, in her husband's company in the long, quiet hours between darkness and dawn, Shahrazad began to feel a thing she had not expected: Perhaps, at last, she had found the place where she belonged.

But even though the feelings grew with each day that passed, neither Shahrayar nor Shahrazad spoke them aloud. Each was uncertain how to put what their hearts felt into words, and so they waited for the heart of the other to reveal itself.

Each day, the king sent a herald to announce to the people that he would spare his wife for one day longer, and the whole kingdom rejoiced. But, as the days wore on and began to blend together like drops of rain streaming down a leaf, fewer and fewer people came to hear Shahrazad's life proclaimed in the palace courtyard. Finally the day came when none appeared at all. For people had ceased to wonder whether the queen might live, but came to take it for granted that she would do so.

And thus it came to pass that the only ones for whom Shahrazad's life continued to be a wonder were those whom it most closely concerned: Nur al-Din Hasan, the vizier, her father. Dinarzad, her sister. Shahrayar, the king, her husband. Shahrazad herself. And also young 'Ajib, who had once been a prince in his own right, though this was a thing that those around him still did not know.

Then during the peace and quiet of these days a rumor began. Though it came to roost in many ears, then flew from many mouths, none could say for sure just how it started. For that is the way of such things, both their weakness and their power.

And the rumor all heard, then spoke, was this: The reason Shahrayar prolonged the life of Shahrazad, his queen, was not that he was gracious and beneficent (though, the fact that he was both these things was surely so). No! The reason King Shahrayar spared the life of Shahrazad the queen was because, with her stories, she had woven a great enchantment around him. In short, the king was bewitched.

A very dangerous situation indeed. One that could not be allowed to go on.

It was the king's own chamberlain who added these final words himself. For no sooner had the rumor found a place first in his ears, then in his mouth, than it found its way into his heart and made itself a home. Long had the chamberlain nursed a grudge against the vizier, for Nur al-Din Hasan had been honored by two kings in succession, and it seemed to the chamberlain that he himself had yet to be honored or even appreciated by just one.

The honors bestowed upon the vizier left none for him, or so the chamberlain had always thought. And furthermore, he thought that it was unjust that this was so. For was he not charged with at least as important a duty as the vizier who, as a councilor, did little more than talk when all was said and done? The chamberlain was charged with guarding the life of the king, even at the cost of his own.

How had it come to pass, then, that the vizier should be honored and the chamberlain ignored? Never had the chamberlain been able to answer this question, for never once had he perceived that it was due to a lack within himself. And so he had failed to place the blame where it belonged—at his own door. But with each passing day the king continued to spare Shahrazad's life, the chamberlain began to perceive an important truth: His misfortunes, as well as the king's, had the same cause. And that cause was none other than the vizier himself, and his daughter, Shahrazad.

For the more the chamberlain thought about it, the more certain he became that the vizier and his daughter were plotting together. It only made sense, after all. What father would consent to put forward his own daughter to be the bride of the king, knowing she must die? Even the vizier could not be so unnatural, or so the chamberlain surmised.

Surely that left just one explanation: The vizier and his daughter were plotting together to overthrow King Shahrayar.

First, they would weaken his mind with magic. Indeed, this had already begun. For there must be sorcery at work in Shahrazad's stories. Had they not caused the king to repudiate what he himself had proclaimed must be so? What else did Shahrazad's stories do but prolong her own life by holding the king in thrall?

And the longer she lived, the greater the danger to Shahrayar must be, for the more potent her spell over him would become.

When the brothers of the former queen heard this (for of course it was they who had started the rumors in the first place), they could hardly contain their secret delight. For now their rumors were impossible to separate from those of the chamberlain, and the claim that Shahrazad and her father had bewitched the king came to roost in every ear, then flew from every mouth until the whole of Shahrayar's kingdom rang with the sound.

And from there it was but a simple step to the one the brothers hoped would give them their revenge. And so they took the gift the chamberlain had unknowingly bestowed upon them and to it added one final touch.

Soon all began to whisper that if Shahrayar could not show himself stronger than his wife's enchantment by putting her to death, it would be proof that Shahrazad's magic ruled his mind. In which case, Shahrayar would no longer be a true king and could not be considered fit to govern.

And so, by degrees, though neither of them could remember from whose mouth they first had heard it, the rumors reached Shahrazad and Shahrayar. But from there they went no further, for neither could bring themselves to speak of it to the other. And in this way did doubt begin to cloud the bright things that had been growing in their hearts.

When Shahrazad learned what the people were saying, her first thoughts were not for herself, but for her father and for Shahrayar. For, like her mother before her, Shahrazad recognized that the love of the people was a thing that she had never truly possessed. She had only provoked their curiosity.

And now, it seemed, their fear. And so Shahrazad knew fear also. For in her quest to save the heart of the king she had two main allies: time and her skill as a storyteller. So tightly were these two woven together that disaster must surely follow if they were unraveled from each other before the proper moment. But when that moment would come, Shahrazad could not know. She knew only that it had not yet arrived.

And so she trembled as she stood in a pool of bright sunshine, for the very first time finding no joy in the coming of the morning. Her blind eyes were turned toward a window although they gazed only inward, and still she saw nothing. She trembled for the things already said as well as for the things she might not now have time to say. Things she had not known that she would long for. For, in her desire to save Shahrayar's heart, she had forgotten that she must also contend for her own.

And it was in this fearful state of mind that Shahrayar found Shahrazad.

He had heard the rumors just that morning. Though his first reaction had been rage, it did not take long for fear to creep into his heart just as it had into Shahrazad's. Suddenly he remembered the words of the boy, 'Ajib, who had proclaimed there must be magic in Shahrazad's story. And if even he could perceive this possibility, being but a child ...

But whereas Shahrazad's fear had been a path that carried her straight to her husband's and father's doors, Shahrayar's fear was like a great jewel that sparkles in the light. Sharp-edged, and so multifaceted as to be all but blinding.

Everywhere his fear compelled him to look, it seemed Shahrayar saw his own reflection. Each one the face of a man who had made a different decision in his time of greatest crisis. But which face was his true reflection, which deed should be his true act, these things Shahrayar could not see, for his own face blinded him.

And so, in their fear, Shahrazad and Shahrayar increased their own danger, though they did not do so knowingly. For, each in his or her own way, both looked in the wrong direction: not inward, but outward. In the moment when they most needed to recall it, both forgot the first queen's prophecy.

Only by knowing what was in their hearts and being unafraid to have it known could all be made right once more. And so the final chapters in the story, which they were weaving together themselves, came to be set in motion.

When Shahrayar entered his quarters and saw Shahrazad standing before the window, he felt himself struck by so many different emotions that he could do nothing but stand and behold her.

What is she thinking? he wondered. Did she know of the rumors that filled the land? The ones that proclaimed her a sorceress and called for her death? If she did, would she even tell him?

For it came to Shahrayar suddenly as he gazed upon his wife that she was still almost completely a mystery to him in spite of the way her voice had found a home inside him. Her voice, yes. That he thought he knew. But her mind, her heart, those things were still unknown and were as deep and fathomless as any well. And just as vital to his life as water, or so Shahrayar was coming to suspect.

What does Shahrazad truly contain? he wondered. Was she pure, as he had originally perceived her to be? Or was she tainted, as the rumors now insisted she must be? For in this uncertainty, more than anything else, did Shahrayar's fear distract and blind him. And so he turned to the wrong place to find the answers to his questions: not to his own heart, or even to their hearts together, but to Shahrazad's heart alone.

If only she would reveal herself to me, all would be well, he thought, never stopping to remember that to reveal one's heart alone is a difficult thing, perhaps the most difficult thing of all.

So, though he had come to his quarters with some vague notion of telling her what he had learned so he could weigh her reaction to it, when Shahrayar opened his mouth to speak, no word of the rumors came out. Instead he said, "What do you see when you gaze out the window, Shahrazad?"

At the sound of her husband's voice, a ripple passed through Shahrazad. For the first time since they had been wed, she had not sensed his presence the moment he entered the room, so far away from the place her body was had she traveled in her thoughts. Her journey had not been a pleasant one. Never had she felt so blind.

"I do not see," she said. "Instead I . . . wonder."

"What do you wonder?" asked Shahrayar.

Shahrazad was silent for a moment, as if framing her reply. "Whether the great world outside is as I remember it," she said at last. "I have not been outside the palace since I was a child."

At this, it seemed to Shahrayar that his fear and confusion vanished, and he saw his way clear once more.

"Come with me," he said on impulse, and he moved to Shahrazad's side and took her by the hand. "Let us go out together."

At his words, Shahrazad felt her heart give a great leap, even as her words faltered. "But . . . the people—"

Ah! Shahrayar thought. *So she knows.* But it mattered less than he had thought it did.

"Let us not worry about them," he said. "Just for a little while. I am tired of seeing you only in the lamplight. Come with me into the sunlight, Shahrazad."

And Shahrazad answered steadily, though Shahrayar could feel the way her fingers trembled in his.

"I would like to feel the sun upon my face with you beside me."

Shahrayar raised her hand, pressed his lips against her palm and felt the way her trembling spread throughout her body.

"Come, then. Let us go."

❖Fifteen❖

A SUNLIGHT STORY

And so Shahrayar and Shahrazad left the palace. They took no retainers, wore no fine robes. They did not even pause to tell the vizier that they were going. Indeed, Shahrayar sent the vizier on an errand that would keep him busy until after nightfall. In this way, he hoped he and Shahrazad might leave the palace and return again with no one the wiser. He did not intend deception in this, merely to travel as another man might. For this one day, if no day else, to leave the cares of government behind him.

So he wrapped Shahrazad in a cloak from head to foot, lifted her upon his horse, then vaulted up behind her. She leaned back against his body. Shahrayar stretched his arms around on either side of her to hold the reins. Both remained silent. In this way, they passed through the least impressive of the palace gates and, at length, through the gates of Shahrayar's city itself and out into the desert beyond. Unremarked upon, unheralded, unnoticed.

"Where are you taking me?" Shahrazad inquired.

Shahrayar laughed suddenly, surprising them both.

"I am not going to tell you. Let the tale of this journey be as much a mystery to you as the tales you spin are to me."

"As the king commands," answered Shahrazad, her tone as light as his own. "Meantime, with your permission, I will enjoy the wind in my hair."

"Gladly," said Shahrayar.

So Shahrazad shook back her cloak and Shahrayar spurred the horse forward till they flew along the sand, Shahrazad's long, dark hair like banners in the wind around them. How long they traveled she never knew, for it was a thing she had ceased to care about. She cared only about the warmth of the sun on her face, the breath of the wind through her hair. The rhythm of the horse as its strides came together and apart, together and apart. And, always, the feel of Shahrayar's arms around her.

After some time, she heard him speak to the horse, and the pace of their travel slowed, then came to a halt, and her hair settled down around her shoulders.

"This is the place," Shahrayar said.

Shahrazad took a deep breath. "Do I smell water?"

Shahrayar smiled as he slid from the horse, then lifted her down. Though she was steady on her feet, he kept one arm about her shoulders, for he had suddenly discovered how empty his arms could feel without her inside them.

"You do," he replied. Gently, he began to lead her across the sand to where a stand of date palms created a small oasis of shade. "My father brought me here when I was but a boy. I should always know how to find water in the desert, he said. So that when I grew to be king, I might never forget its importance to my subjects."

"Your father was wise. My father always told me I should never take anything essential for granted lest I lose it, but now I see it is probably because yours said it first."

Shahrayar chuckled. They settled beneath the trees, Shahrazad with her back against one great trunk. Shahrayar stretched out and laid his head in her lap.

I am free, he thought. Though he had not known he had felt confined until this moment. He looked up at Shahrazad, who was sitting with her face tipped up to the sun.

"Shahrazad, will you tell me something?"

She did not reply, but merely nodded.

Do you fear to lose me? Have I become so essential to you that you will treasure me always and never take me for granted?

The words quivered upon his tongue, welled straight up from his heart with a heat that left Shahrayar shaking as if he had a fever. But at the last moment, he found he could not pronounce them.

What did it matter if he thought he suddenly saw and understood his own heart? He still could neither see nor understand Shahrazad's. And in what he could not see lay pain and danger, or so he thought.

And so he did not ask the questions that were in his heart. Never stopping to think that in refusing, he kept his own heart as much a secret to Shahrazad as hers was to him. And so both stayed locked up tight, the hopes and needs in them unspoken.

"Will you tell me a story?" he asked instead.

"A story!" exclaimed Shahrazad. "But Maju's trunk is in the palace."

"Can you not find a story in any piece of cloth?" Shahrayar inquired.

"I do not know," Shahrazad answered truthfully. "For I have never tried it. But I suppose it would be possible, for it is the finding of the story that is the true storyteller's art, or so Maju always told me."

"Then we could try it," Shahrayar insisted.

"Yes," Shahrazad acknowledged. "We could try. What piece of cloth would you have me decipher?"

"This one."

On impulse Shahrayar reached out and captured one of Shahrazad's wrists in his hand. With the other he pushed back her sleeve to reveal the small scrap of fabric he had noticed she always wore there. Never had he seen her without it, not even as she slept. He wondered what significance it had for her, and also what tale the cloth might hold.

"You wish to know the tale of this?" Shahrazad asked, her tone astonished. Her heart began to beat swift as a bird's wing within her breast. What did it mean that Shahrayar had been drawn to the only thing she wore that had come from Maju?

"I do," Shahrayar said. "Where did it come from?"

"Maju gave it to me long ago," Shahrazad replied. "In a time of trial and sorrow. I do not think she intended it as a gift, but I have treasured it always."

"Then if it comes from Maju, surely there must be a tale within it," Shahrayar said.

And Shahrazad answered, "I do not know, but since you wish it, I will try to find it."

"Thank you," said Shahrayar. He sat up, and with careful fingers, untied the piece of cloth from her wrist. But when he spread it out he exclaimed, "But surely this cloth has been stained with blood, Shahrazad!"

"It has been," she replied. "With mine when I was just a child."

And at her words, a memory came to Shahrayar. Of himself, also a child, concealed within the branches of a pomegranate tree, watching a young Shahrazad's wounds being bound up by her mother as the young girl poured the bitterness and grief from her heart.

"Why would you keep such a thing?" Shahrayar asked, though he thought he knew, for now he remembered what else had happened on that day long ago: The thing that she had vowed.

"So that I might remember my own promises to myself," Shahrazad said, confirming what Shahrayar surmised. "And also, that I might have some token of my mother. These are the tales I have added to this cloth," she went on, as if to forestall any further questions. "Now let us see what was there to start out."

So saying, she stretched out her hand and Shahrayar placed the piece of cloth upon her palm. Shahrazad ran her fingers back and forth across the old stained piece of silk as if she had never touched it before.

"Ah!" she said at last. "It seems that you are right, my lord. A story may be found anywhere, if one is willing to search for it. The one that I have found here is called . . ."

❖Sixteen❖

THE TALE OF THE FISHERMAN, THE PRINCE, AND THE WATER BEARER'S DAUGHTER

"Once, in a land much like our own, there lived a poor water bearer who had but one child, and that was a daughter. His wife had died in giving birth, and since the water bearer was too poor to remarry, father and daughter lived all alone, though they were not lonely. For such was their affection for one another, that even though it was not filled with fine things, to them their home seemed always full to overflowing.

"As the years went by, the child grew to be a young woman who possessed rich gifts in spite of her poor estate. And those gifts numbered four and were as follows: her kind heart, her beauty, her bravery, and her honesty.

"One day it happened that the prince of this land, who was something of a ne'er-do-well, interested more in looking like a prince than in acting like one, decided to elude his tutors and have a great adventure in the city which surrounded his palace. But, though he successfully managed to make his escape, it did not take long for him to lose his way once he had done so. For he did not know the city at all, being greatly sheltered and having only gone out previously with his servants and retainers to guide him.

"Being lost, he should have stood still and waited to be found. But, being foolish, he did not. Instead he began to wander. And so, after many hours he found himself in a rough portion of the city where things might have ended very badly for him indeed. For in his fine garments, with jewels flashing from almost every finger, it was not long before he was set upon by a band of thieves. They knocked him to the ground and dragged him into a nearby alley.

"But, having secured their prize, the thieves fell to doing what thieves often do, for they have no honor: They quarreled amongst themselves. Some of the band were all for cutting off the young man's fingers—the better to obtain the rich jewels he wore. Others argued that it would be better to truss him up on a spit and suspend him over a pit of hot coals. In this way they could force him to reveal the name of his family and ransom him for more money than they had ever dreamed of.

"The prince had just reached the point where he was considering groveling in a very unprincelike manner when the thieves were interrupted. The water bearer and his daughter were making their way home and took a shortcut through the alley.

"Now, you might suppose, as the prince had, that

a band of thieves would find little to fear from a water bearer who was not as young as he used to be, and his only child who was a daughter. But if you had supposed such a thing, you would have been as mistaken as the prince was, for in that rough place the water bearer's strength was well known and commanded much respect. Had he not spent his life carrying burdens too heavy for others?

"And to the father's strength of body, there was added the daughter's bravery. She was quick as an eel and afraid of nothing.

"At the sight of the water bearer and his daughter, the thieves fled, leaving the prince alone. At first the prince feared he had met with ruffians much worse than the first, for who else could have put such desperate creatures to flight? But his fears were soon allayed when the water bearer and his daughter treated him with kindness. They took him to their home and tended to his wounds. The prince gazed about him in wonder, for never had he seen such a humble abode. Although it was clean, it had but one room, and that a small one. How could people of such goodness live in such surroundings?

"As the water bearer's daughter bound up his wounds, the prince could not help but notice her loveliness, and thus he spoke to her. 'Tell me how it is that a flower as beautiful as you can flourish in such a harsh and desperate place. Surely you belong in a well-tended garden.'

"'I have grown as I am exactly where I was planted,'

she replied. 'Is it not then the case that I am so because of my surroundings?'

"'You are wise as well as beautiful, I see,' the prince said gallantly.

"'And your mouth is as a honeycomb,' the girl answered honestly. 'What falls from it is sweet, but I fear the taste will not last long.'

"'Not so!' cried the prince, for like a bee, her words had stung him. He was unaccustomed to his flattery failing, and he had wanted to make a good impression upon the water bearer's daughter. 'If you knew my true identity, you would not say such a thing,' he went on, for it seemed to him that she must take him more seriously when she knew who he was.

"'Very well,' the girl said, not yet particularly impressed. 'Who are you?'

"'I am Prince Khasib, and when my father dies I shall be king over all this land.'

"Upon hearing this news, the water bearer's daughter fell to her knees in astonishment. And her father, coming into the room just then, dropped his water skins so that their precious contents spilled out upon the floor—a thing he had not done once in all his years.

"Their reactions both pleased and vexed Prince Khasib. Certainly it was wonderful to be so admired, but he had not wished to inspire fear. He wanted the water bearer's daughter to look upon him with favor, as he looked upon her.

"'Majesty,' the water bearer gasped. 'We are honored

by your presence in our humble home. But this is too rough a place for one so fine as you. Let me send a messenger to the palace at once.'

"And so the prince agreed. But while the water bearer was out finding a boy to run to the palace, the prince plucked the jewel from his little finger and gave it to the water bearer's daughter with these words:

"'If ever you have need of me, bring this and come to the palace.'

"'Sire, I will,' the girl replied, though in her heart she could not imagine when such a time might arise. She was certain she would never see the handsome prince again.

"Now, I probably do not need to tell you (but I will do so anyway, for the story demands it) that things we cannot imagine often have a strange way of happening in spite of us. And so it was with the water bearer's daughter. Not long after this, on his way home from carrying water to the home of a rich courtier, the water bearer was seized and thrown into prison without a word of explanation. Nothing his daughter could do would secure his release. Indeed, his jailers hinted that he might not be allowed to live much longer. Strong and courageous though she was, the water bearer's daughter was soon close to despair.

"But before she could give way to it completely, she remembered the ring the prince had given her and his words at their parting. So she dressed herself in her finest garments and set out for the palace.

"Now, the distance from the home of a water bearer and his daughter to a prince's palace is a great one. So great, that by the time the water bearer's daughter had traveled it, her finest garments were covered with dust, and the hours allotted for audiences were nearly over. The palace guards took one look at her and turned her away.

"'Come back tomorrow.'

"'But I must see Prince Khasib as soon as possible,' the water bearer's daughter cried. 'See! I have his token. If ever I have need of him, he commanded I should bring this to the palace.' And with these words, she produced the ring and held it out.

"At this, the palace guards began to take her more seriously. Not because they believed a word she said, but because they felt sure the ring must have been stolen. They were just on the verge of hauling the water bearer's daughter off to prison too when, to the surprise of all, a court lady who happened to be passing by intervened.

"'Fools!' she exclaimed angrily. 'Can you not see that this girl speaks the truth? Do you not recognize the Prince's mark?'

"And upon close examination, her claim proved to be true. For on the inside of the band, so cunningly placed that only when you gazed into the jewel itself could you see it, was the official mark of Prince Khasib.

"At this, the guards began to be afraid that *they*

would be the ones thrown into prison, and so they let the water bearer's daughter enter the palace at once. The court lady went so far as to escort her to the audience chamber, the water bearer's daughter expressing her appreciation for the lady's kindness the entire way.

"'Think nothing of it,' the court lady said with a wave of her perfumed hand. 'But remember well this good deed that I have done you. Perhaps you may do one for me someday.'

"'If ever it is within my power to do you good, I will,' the water bearer's daughter promised. And with that, they reached the audience chamber. Here again the court lady exerted herself on the water bearer's daughter's behalf.

"'Here is one who begs an audience with Prince Khasib,' she cried in a loud voice. 'She comes bearing his token. Let her be heard.' With that, she moved forward, bringing the water bearer's daughter with her. And so they came to Prince Khasib.

"Glad as he was to see the water bearer's daughter once again, seeing the two women together was not so pleasing to Prince Khasib. For the token he had given to one had been a gift to him from the other. In truth, the ring he had bestowed upon the water bearer's daughter had not truly been his to give: It had been a gift to him from the fine court lady who wished to win his favor. In short, the situation had all the makings of a fine muddle.

"Nor was this all, for beneath his handsome

countenance and gallant manners, there lived a darkness in the heart of Prince Khasib. It was he who was responsible for the water bearer's imprisonment. Until he gave the word, the water bearer would not be released. And all so that the prince could look upon the water bearer's daughter once more, to discover if she was as lovely as he remembered. And to impress upon her that her happiness was in his hands.

"But the water bearer's daughter knew nothing of this. And so she cast herself to the ground before Prince Khasib and said, 'Hear me, O great and shining Prince! I come as you have said I might, bearing your token, to beg for your help in my hour of greatest need.'

"The first of the matters that had weighed on Prince Khasib's mind was thus easily dispatched. For, even streaked with dust and in despair, the water bearer's daughter was just as lovely as he had at first perceived.

"'What would you have me do?' he asked, pleased to have her acknowledge her need of him so quickly. 'Rise and tell me.'

"So the water bearer's daughter rose to her feet and said, 'My father has been imprisoned for a cause I cannot discover. I fear his life may be forfeit. I beg you to order his release, and so spare both his life and my own. For it is not possible that I should live without him.'

"Now, this was not precisely what Prince Khasib wished to hear. If she could not live without someone, it should be him. 'Yet surely he must die some-day,' he countered.

"'As God shall will it,' the water bearer's daughter acknowledged. 'But I greatly fear that what has befallen him is, instead, the will of man.'

"'If I might be so bold, Highness,' the court lady spoke up suddenly. 'I may be able to suggest a way to determine whether the imprisonment of this maid's father be just or no.'

"At this, Prince Khasib perceived that he was growing more unhappy by the minute, for this inter-ruption was not at all to his liking. It was hardly pos-sible the court lady would have the best interests of the water bearer's daughter at heart. She was more likely to wish some mischief upon her. But Prince Khasib had no choice but to listen to what she had to say, for she had caught the attention of his courtiers.

"'Speak,' he commanded.

"'I would propose a test,' the court lady said. 'A trial of some sort. Command this maid to do a thing that all others before her have failed to accomplish. If she succeeds, you will know her cause is just.'

"At her words, a murmuring of appreciation filled the audience chamber, a counterbalance to the dread filling Prince Khasib's heart.

"'What might such a task be?' he inquired.

"'Gracious!' the court lady exclaimed with a becoming blush. 'How should I know? Yet I have heard . . .' Her voice trailed off, and in spite of himself,

Prince Khasib leaned forward on his seat of ivory.

"'What?'

"'I have heard of a treasure that rests at the bottom of the ocean,' the court lady went on. 'A treasure so remarkable, only one who possesses both strength of body and purity of heart has even the slightest hope of finding it. Many have tried, but so far, all have failed. Surely this would be a fitting gift to bestow upon a prince to ransom the life of a much-loved father.'

"At these words, the swell of wonder from the courtiers within the audience chamber grew so great that Prince Khasib perceived an astonishing thing: His mind was already made up. For to refuse such a remarkable request would be unthinkable. And so he turned back to the water bearer's daughter and said, 'Find this treasure for me. When I hold it in my hand, I will have proof your cause is just and free your father. Not only that, on that day, I will make you my bride. For any who can find such a treasure must surely be a treasure herself and fit to be a prince's consort.'

"And with that, the prince smiled at the court lady. *See what happens to all those who would try to outsmart me,* he thought.

"But the water bearer's daughter hardly noticed the prince's offer to make her his bride. She was too filled with dismay at the task he had set her, for it seemed to her that it was impossible. She had never even seen the ocean, did not even know where it might be found. But she rallied her courage, for she was her father's only hope, and she knew she must be strong. So she bowed low before the prince and said, 'Majesty, may your will be done.'

"With her words, the day's audiences were over, and the water bearer's daughter returned home. There, she changed her finest garments for her most sensible clothes. Into a knapsack she placed a loaf of bread and some dried figs, which was all the food she had in the house. She filled one of her father's water skins and was just on the point of setting out when she heard a knock upon her door. Opening it, she discovered the court lady who had helped her get into the palace.

"'Forgive me,' the court lady said, casting her eyes down modestly. 'But, after you left the audience chamber, I had you followed. I feel responsible for the fact that you must undertake such an arduous quest, for had I not spoken—'

"'You must not blame yourself,' the water bearer's daughter interrupted swiftly. 'I would do anything to save my father.'

"The court lady raised her eyes and gazed into those of the water bearer's daughter as if searching for something. After several moments, she said, 'You truly love him.'

"'With all my heart.'

"'I am sorry for it,' the court lady said, taking them both by surprise. 'For your way must surely be difficult and long. You may fail. Your father may still die.'

"'I will not fail,' the water bearer's daughter vowed. 'But worse than failing is not to try at all. For then there can be no hope of success.'

"At these words, the court lady gestured to the two servants who had accompanied her. 'Then take these, and may success follow.' The servants placed a basket and a roll of parchment at the water bearer's daughter's feet. Then they bowed low, and all three departed.

"Unrolling the parchment, the water bearer's daughter discovered a map like a jigsaw puzzle, showing how her own country fit into those around it until, at last, the land ended at a great ocean. The distance between where she would begin, and where she must end was so great, it made her bones ache just to study it. But taking careful note of the direction in which she needed to travel, she rolled the map up again and tucked it into her knapsack, saying to herself, *There is no sense on dwelling on what cannot be altered.*

"Opening the basket, she discovered a pair of shoes made of iron. They seemed a strange choice for such a long journey, but she supposed they had one virtue: They would not wear out. So she sat down upon the ground, removed her sandals, and slipped her feet into the iron shoes. They were so heavy, she could barely lift her feet to walk. But she said to herself, *I am not afraid to work hard. Has not my father done so all his life? Besides, every step I take will bring me closer to the moment he is free once more.*

"And so, shouldering her knapsack, the water bearer's daughter set off."

❖Seventeen❖

HOW THE WATER BEARER'S DAUGHTER FINDS THE FISHERMAN, THE TREASURE, AND HER HEART. AND HOW THE STORY FINDS ITS END. IN THAT ORDER.

"*H*ow many days and nights, how the days and nights stretched out to weeks and the weeks to months and maybe even years, is not recorded in the cloth," Shahrazad's voice continued softly. "But this much I can tell you:

"The water bearer's daughter had walked so long, her hair had turned as white as a noonday sky. So far the heels and toes of her iron shoes were worn clean through so that the sand ran in one end and out the other, before she stood at last upon the shore of a vast and swirling blue-green ocean.

"But, though her heart rejoiced to reach her destination at last, it quailed also. For now that she was here, the water bearer's daughter realized several bitter things all at once: She did not know what form the treasure she was looking for might take, and there was no one she might ask, for she was quite alone. And she had remembered suddenly that she could not swim. How then could she hope to find a treasure at the bottom of the ocean?

"The bitterness of these things struck her with such force, her legs gave way and she fell to her knees, soaking her skirts with ocean foam. And there the water bearer's daughter might finally have given up hope when, through eyes grown dim with tears as salty as the great ocean itself, she beheld a sail dancing upon the horizon. The longer she watched, the larger it became, until she could clearly perceive a small boat with a single occupant.

"*I can at least ask this fisherman,* she thought. So she got to her feet and waited patiently upon the shore. But the longer she waited, the more concerned the water bearer's daughter became. For as she watched and waited, the wind came up and the sky grew crowded with clouds as fierce and dark as any she had seen. Without warning, a great needle of light shot down from the sky. It struck so near the boat, the water bearer's daughter swore she smelled scorched wood. With a shout, the fisherman threw himself overboard.

"The water bearer's daughter never even hesitated. Later, it seemed to her she simply moved, with no conscious thought at all. In spite of the fact that she could not swim a stroke, she kicked off what remained of her iron shoes and waded out into the thrashing water.

"It seethed about her, agitated as the brew of a witch's cauldron. After no more than a few struggling steps, the water bearer's daughter felt her feet slip, then leave the bottom. Still, she never faltered, her determination to save the fisherman as great as her need to save her father.

"One wave struck her. Then another. And another. Until the water bearer's daughter's eyes stung with salt, her mouth choked with seawater. But still, she pushed against the waves with all her might, reaching out through the water. On the fourth wave, she felt something brush against her outstretched hands. Something with fingers that reached to meet hers and clung having found them. Sobbing now, the water bearer's daughter held on with one hand, and with the other, reached back toward the shore.

"Again and again she reached. Each time, the strength of her determination brought the land a little closer. Until at last she felt the earth beneath her feet. A few more steps brought her out of the water. And with her, the fisherman, for it was his hand she held fast in her own. Together, they collapsed to the sand, and as they did so, the storm ended as abruptly as it had begun, and the sun shone down upon them, bright and strong.

"'Thank you,' the fisherman said as soon as he was able. 'If not for your courage, my life would have been lost.'

"'Oh, surely not,' the water bearer's daughter answered. 'For you are . . .'

"But here, a strange thing happened. Without warning, a great heaviness seized the water bearer's daughter in all her limbs, as if every step of her long journey had suddenly come to inhabit her body all at the same moment. Her vision darkened until she could not see the fisherman clearly, though he lay beside her. She blinked her eyes once, twice. The third time, her lids stayed closed, and she remembered nothing more.

"She awoke to a warm darkness. She pulled in a breath and found the air scented with smoke from a driftwood fire. She stirred and realized she was covered in a scratchy blanket from feet to chin.

"'So you're awake at last,' the voice of the fisherman said. 'That is good, for I feared I might have lost you.'

"'I am not lost,' the water bearer's daughter replied. And with this, she sat up and looked around her.

"She was in a small cottage made of wood, its roof thatched with the reeds that grew out of the great dunes bordering the ocean. There was a hole in the roof, and through it drifted the driftwood smoke. Though another might have considered it small and poor, the water bearer's daughter could see that the cottage had been well kept, much like the home she shared with her father. And so she felt not scornful or afraid to awaken in a place she did not know, but comfortable and at home.

"Over a pot above the fire, the fisherman stirred something that made the water bearer's daughter's mouth water.

"'What are you making?' she inquired.

"'Seaweed soup,' the fisherman answered. 'It will help to make you strong once more.' So saying, he filled a bowl. As he leaned over the fire, its light played over his features, and the water bearer's daughter felt her breath catch as she beheld him clearly for the very first time.

"Never had she seen a man so ugly.

"His face was lined as if creased by the wind, pitted as if scarred by the salt in the seawater. With his gaze downcast, the water bearer's daughter could not see the color of his eyes. His hands were as wide across as one of her legs. But they cradled her bowl of soup as gently as if it were a bird's nest filled with hatchlings.

"*There is kindness in him*, she thought.

"And so, though her heart beat a little faster at his approach, she took the bowl of soup from him without spilling a drop, for her hands did not tremble. And she said to him, 'I thank you for your kindness.'

"At her words, the fisherman started. 'You are the first who has ever seen it,' he said, and he smiled. When he did this, the water bearer's daughter discovered that it was possible to forget his great ugliness, for his kindness was the only thing she saw.

"'Eat your soup,' he said. 'Then, if you are not too weary, tell me how you have come to be in this place, for I think that you are far from home.'

"'I am, indeed,' the water bearer's daughter said, 'though this cottage reminds me of it.'

"At this, though he did not speak, the fisherman

smiled once more. The water bearer's daughter ate her soup, then told him of all that had lately befallen her.

"'I have heard of this treasure you seek,' the fisherman said when her tale was done. 'It may be that I can even show you where it lies. But seeking is not the same as finding. Many have come before you, and all have failed.'

"'I will not fail,' the water bearer's daughter answered firmly. 'I will succeed, for I must save my father.'

"'In the morning, we shall see,' the fisherman said. 'Sleep, now.' So saying, he took her empty bowl from her, then tucked her in once more. The water bearer's daughter was asleep by the time the blanket reached her chin.

"In the middle of the night, she awoke to find the fire had died down low. The fisherman sat beside it, weaving a great net, his eyes glowing bright as the coals.

"In the morning, her strength restored, the water bearer's daughter followed the fisherman down to the water. There they climbed into his boat, and the fisherman plied the oars. Today the sea was as smooth as honey. When they reached a spot in the ocean that looked the same as any other to the water bearer's daughter, the fisherman lifted the oars from the water.

"'The treasure that you seek is down below us. To find it, you must dive to the bottom.'

"Though she had never done such a thing before,

the water bearer's daughter rose. 'Then that is what I will do,' she vowed.

"'Keep your head down,' the fisherman advised. 'Reach with your arms for the bottom.'

"'I will,' the water bearer's daughter said, and with no more ado, she dove over the side.

"Down, down, down she went, through water so smooth it felt like silk, always keeping her head aimed downward and reaching with her arms for the bottom. Her heartbeats began to pound in her ears. Then at last, she saw what she was searching for. The sand at the bottom of the ocean was white and pure as milk, but whiter still were the bones resting on top of it.

"*These are the ones who came before me and failed*, the water bearer's daughter thought. Scattered among the bones was a treasure such as she had never dreamed of: Jewels of every size and shape. Gold coins too numerous to count. Surely something here would ransom her father. The question was, what?

"Just when the water bearer's daughter thought her breath would last no longer, she caught a dazzle from the corner of her eye. A ruby, big as her fist, nestled in the right eye socket of a half-buried skull. She snatched it up, then shot toward the surface, breaking through the water at the last possible moment, desperately pulling breath into her lungs. She felt the fisherman reach down and lift her up into the boat.

"'Well?' he said after giving her a chance to catch her breath. 'What have you found?'

"The water bearer's daughter opened her hand to reveal the ruby. To her horror and dismay, the fisherman snatched it from her and heaved it back into the ocean.

"'You will not save your father with that,' he said. 'You must try again tomorrow.'

"With that, he spoke not another word, but rowed them back to shore. That night, much was as it had been the night before. The water bearer's daughter awakened just once, in the dead of night. She saw the fisherman sitting by the fire, weaving a great net by the fireside, his eyes glowing bright as the coals.

"Now began a series of days when the exact same thing happened. The fisherman fished while the water bearer's daughter dove. But each time she retrieved what she hoped was the treasure she sought, the fisherman would declare it useless and throw it back into the sea once more.

"As the days passed, the water bearer's daughter grew more and more desperate. The rich jewels adorning the bottom of the ocean began to lose their shine. Though they might be valuable, they were not precious. And within the water bearer's daughter's heart was a growing certainty that the only thing that could ransom her father was a treasure beyond price. But she did not yet see what it was.

"She began staying beneath the waves longer and longer, pushing herself to the limits of her breath before she made her choice. Until finally the day came when she brought up nothing at all. For she had left her choice too late. To choose would be to drown. On that day, after he had lifted her into the boat, the fisherman said nothing at all. But that night, when the water bearer's daughter awoke in the dead of night, the fisherman said, 'Have you ever wondered how all those bones came to be at the bottom of the ocean?'

"'Never,' answered the water bearer's daughter. 'For surely it is obvious. They are the bones of those who tried before me.'

"'Tried and failed,' the fisherman reminded her. 'Do you know why?'

"Before today, the water bearer's daughter might not have had an answer. But now she thought she understood, and so she replied, 'The day came when they could not choose, and so they drowned.'

"'That is so,' the fisherman said with a nod. 'But that is not all. They did not know how to look, trusting only the eyes of the mind. But the treasure you seek will never be found that way.'

"'How, then?' the water bearer's daughter asked.

"'With the eyes of the heart,' the fisherman replied. 'They alone will show you the treasure you seek. If you fail in this, you will suffer the same fate as all the others.'

"'I will not fail,' the water bearer's daughter said, just as she had that first morning.

"'We shall see,' the fisherman replied. 'Sleep now. One way or the other, tomorrow will be your last dive.'

"The following morning found the fisherman and the water bearer's daughter in the fisherman's small boat once more. The fisherman fished. The water bearer's daughter dove over the side. But even though she did so again and again, she could find nothing she thought might ransom her father, for now all seemed changed. Nothing looked as it had before.

"Although she had thought all the rest of the night about the fisherman's words, the water bearer's daughter had not been able to find the hidden meaning in them. How did one see with the heart and not the mind? The more times she dove, the more frustrated the water bearer's daughter became. And now, a terrible fear seized her for the very first time.

"She was going to fail, as all the others before her had. Both she and her father would die.

"Late in the day, she lay in the boat, gathering up her breath for one last dive. All through the long hours, the fisherman had remained silent. But he spoke now. 'You should trust yourself more. You already have the gift to see as you need to, you just don't recognize it.'

"'How can I have a gift and not recognize it?' the water bearer's daughter asked, her tone waspish. *And by the way, I tire of you talking in riddles*, she thought. But out of gratitude for all he had done for her, she did not say this aloud.

"'By not understanding it for the gift it is,' the fisherman replied with a smile. Exactly as if he had heard what she had not spoken as well as what she had. 'Now let me ask you something: How did you look upon my face and yet see that one as ugly as I could also be kind?'

"'I don't know, exactly,' the water bearer's daughter said. 'I just looked and saw it.'

"'Then that is what you must do to find the treasure,' the fisherman said.

"'Very well,' the water bearer's daughter answered. 'I will try.'

"'Then it is time for your last dive.'

"The fisherman pulled her to her feet. The water bearer's daughter clasped his hand in hers for just a moment, as if to draw strength from its solidity and size. Then she released it, took one enormous breath, and dove into the ocean.

"Down, down, down she plummeted through water as blue and sparkling as a sapphire, until she reached the shimmering white sand that lay at the ocean's bottom. There she paused, her long hair moving about her. But this time she did not focus on the jewels. Instead, she did a thing her mind insisted made no sense at all: She closed her eyes.

"She felt her hair shifting around her in the ocean's unseen currents. She saw the way the light, filtered through the layers of water, created a rosy glow against the inside of her eyelids. It even seemed to her she felt the heart of the great ocean itself, opening to enfold her in its liquid embrace.

"And then completely without warning, the face

of the fisherman popped into her mind.

"At this, the water bearer's daughter's eyes sprang open, and she knew that she had found the treasure for which she had searched so long and so hard.

"It was a shell, enormous and dark. Encrusted with things whose names she could only guess at. Its scalloped edges looked as sharp as knives. *This shell is like the fisherman,* she thought. For buried deep within it, the water bearer's daughter thought she caught the glimmer of a treasure precious beyond her ability to measure—in spite of its rough and ugly outside.

"With her last ounce of strength, she snatched up the shell, then shot to the surface. The fisherman hauled her into the boat. He waited for her to catch her breath, then asked softly, 'Will you show me what you have found?'

"The water bearer's daughter held out the shell. At the sight of it, the fisherman's great hands trembled, and he shielded his eyes. And it was only in this moment that the water bearer's daughter realized what color they were: the same changeable blue-green as the sea around them.

"'Well done,' the fisherman said. 'For there is more in this than you yet know. But for now it is enough that you have found the thing you came for. Tonight we will sleep, and tomorrow, ransom your father.'

"'But the way is long,' the water bearer's daughter protested. 'It cannot be possible we can ransom him tomorrow.'

"The fisherman took her face between his still-trembling hands. 'Do you trust me?' he asked softly.

"'I trust you,' said the water bearer's daughter.

"'Then believe in me also. For I swear to you that tomorrow your father will be free at last.'

"And the water bearer's daughter's heart was filled with joy. That night, for what she thought would be the very last time, she slept in the fisherman's house. She awoke in the dead of night, as always. The fisherman sat beside the fire, turning the shell over and over in his hands, his eyes glowing as bright as the coals.

"At the sight of this, the water bearer's daughter rose from her bed and went to sit by his side. He wrapped her in his cloak. She rested her head upon his shoulder. There she fell asleep once more. But the fisherman stayed awake all night, for in his head were thoughts that would not let him close his eyes. And so the hours passed until the dawn.

"Just as the first hint of light crept into the sky, the fisherman arose, placed the shell upon the breast of the still-sleeping water bearer's daughter, wrapped both more securely in his cloak, picked her up, stepped out his front door, and closed it behind him. For a moment, he simply stood, looking out upon the ocean. Then, with one strong arm, he took up the net upon which he had labored every night since he had first made the cottage by the sea his home, and he turned his back upon the water.

"In a great swinging arc, he cast the net out, not across the sea, but across the land. The net was so vast, it stretched beyond the horizon. Then the fisherman gathered up the net, took one step forward, and cast it again, beyond the next horizon.

"Again and again, the fisherman cast out his great net and gathered it in. Cast it out and gathered it in. Each time taking one step forward. With each step he took, he brought himself closer to his own destiny and the water bearer's daughter closer to her father. So that by the time she stirred in the fisherman's arms and he set her down, they were but a street away from Prince Khasib's palace.

"When the water bearer's daughter realized where they were, her mouth opened and closed like a fish on the shore, a thing that caused the fisherman to smile.

"'Don't worry about the "how" of this yet,' he said. 'For there will be time to explain all things after we have ransomed your father.'

"'There is no way I can ever thank you enough,' the water bearer's daughter said, finally finding her voice.

"The fisherman raised an eyebrow. 'Do you not think so? But that, too, can wait. Come, let us go to the palace.'

"Great was the amazement of the guards when they saw the water bearer's daughter had returned. For after her departure, word of the deed she would attempt had spread until there was no one in the land who did not know of it. But even though all knew of her, none had expected her to return.

"She was shown to Prince Khasib's great audience chamber at once, the fisherman trailing along behind her. There the water bearer's daughter was astonished to discover that while for her the time had flown while she accomplished her quest, in the palace of Prince Khasib, time had crawled, so that little more than a month had passed since she first set out.

"Though it took him a moment to recognize her, for her feet were bare and covered with sand, and her hair was white as bone, when the prince realized the water bearer's daughter had returned, great was his joy! His courtiers were struck dumb with wonder, then began to talk all at once. The beautiful court lady fainted dead away and had to be revived. In all the confusion, no one noticed the presence of the fisherman at all. He stood at the back of the audience chamber, watching as the water bearer's daughter moved down its great length alone.

"'Sire,' she said as she knelt before Prince Khasib when order had been restored. 'Behold! I have brought you the great treasure you asked for. I place it in your hand, as you bade me. Therefore, I beg you, free my father. Spare his life and mine.'

"'Gladly,' Prince Khasib said as he took the shell from her. He was so carried away by seeing the water bearer's daughter again, he hardly noticed what it was that she had brought him. With a wave of his arm, he sent the captain of his guard to free the water bearer. 'Not only that, I will make preparations for our wedding at once.'

"At these words the courtiers began to cheer so loudly, the court lady had to shriek like a banshee to be heard over them, and the water bearer's daughter's mouth fell open. For the truth was she had forgotten all about Prince Khasib's pledge to marry her if she was successful. She had thought only of saving her father. But now that he mentioned it, she realized that she had no wish to marry the prince at all. In fact, if she had her choice . . .

"'I see no great treasure!' the court lady shouted, interrupting both the courtiers' cries and the water bearer's daughter's thoughts. 'I see only a shell such as anyone might find. Spare her father if you will, but do not marry this common girl, my lord. For I fear she leads you on for some purpose of her own.'

"'Nonsense!' Prince Khasib shouted back. And at his words, a silence fell while all gazed at the shell the water bearer's daughter had brought. 'Though, I must admit you do have a point. I see nothing special in this.'

"*But how can that be?* the water bearer's daughter thought. How could it be that a great prince saw only the surface of a thing, while she, a mere water bearer's daughter saw so much more?

"And then a strange thing happened. For as the water bearer's daughter looked upon Prince Khasib, she saw not only his outward form, she saw what was inside him also. She saw the thing that drove his heart. And it was love, this much was true. But not love for her. It was love of power. Love for himself.

Together, these were so strong, they left no room for loving anything else.

"Turning her eyes upon the court lady, the water bearer's daughter saw into her heart also. And in it there writhed two snakes twined so tightly together, they appeared as one. And they were desire for Prince Khasib, and a will to vanquish any and all who might try to turn this desire aside.

That explains the iron shoes, the water bearer's daughter thought.

"And now the water bearer's daughter turned her back upon Prince Khasib and looked upon the fisherman, knowing that she saw him with the eyes of her heart for the very first time.

How could I have ever thought him ugly? she wondered. For now it seemed to her that he shone as bright and pure as the evening star. From the depths of his heart, her own face smiled back, and she knew in that moment that their hearts were one. Never again was the fisherman anything other than beautiful to her, for never again did she look at him through any other but the eyes of truest love.

"And in this way the water bearer's daughter came to understand that though she had set out to win a treasure for Prince Khasib, she had won a treasure even greater for herself.

"And so she turned to the prince and said, 'The treasure I have brought does not reveal itself in outward form. To discover its worth, you must find the way into its heart. You must see what is inside.'

"But Prince Khasib did not understand her, and, at her words, he grew annoyed. 'How, exactly do you propose I should do that?' he asked, rattling the shell. 'It is locked up tight, and I fear to open it, for the edges are as sharp as knives.'

"'That is a riddle you must solve for yourself,' the water bearer's daughter said. 'You bade me find the treasure and place it in your hand. This I have done. I can do nothing more.'

"'Tell me, or I'll marry another,' the prince threatened, certain this would bring her around.

"But to the astonishment of all, the water bearer's daughter simply smiled. 'I pray you, do, my lord. And let it be the one who first put the idea of this great treasure into your mind. For is it not she who is most truly responsible for bringing it to you? Without her, I would never have set out.'

"And in this way did she repay the court lady for the kindness she had shown her.

"'You are right!' Prince Khasib cried. 'I will marry that lady without delay. And as for you, collect your father and go far from my sight. For a more ungrateful young woman I never have beheld.'

"'It shall be as you say,' the water bearer's daughter promised. And she left the audience chamber, the fisherman at her side. Outside the palace they found the water bearer waiting for them. Great was the happiness of the father and daughter at being reunited! Then the water bearer said to his only child, 'My daughter, who is this who stands so quietly at your side?'

"'This is he who helped me secure your release,' the water bearer's daughter answered. 'And more than that, he is the man I love.'

"'Then I shall love him also,' the water bearer said.

"At these words, the fisherman knelt down before him. 'Once, I was just such a prince as this Khasib,' he said. 'Concerned only with outward form and show. In my arrogance, I once did a powerful sorceress a great wrong. For this, I was condemned to a life of ugliness and loneliness until the day someone should come to love me not for the looks that had once made me so proud, but for the man I had become inside.

"'Though many have looked, your daughter is the only one who ever looked at me and saw me truly. You have pledged your love for me on her word alone. Will you give me her hand in marriage?'

"'Gladly, if this is what my daughter wishes,' the water bearer said.

"'It is,' she vowed.

"'Then one more choice lies before you,' the fisherman said, as he rose to her feet and took her into his arms. 'Now that the spell is broken, will you have me as I am, or as I was? Will you have a fisherman or a prince to be your husband?'

"'That is no choice at all,' the water bearer's daughter said. 'For surely you are both. But if you are asking if I'd like to live in a palace, the answer is no. Let us live in the cottage by the sea.'

"And they did so, and lived in happiness for the rest of their lives. And in this way did the gifts the water bearer's daughter had been born with—her kind heart, her beauty, her bravery, and her honesty—win her treasure precious beyond measure.

"Prince Khasib never did figure out how to open the shell, though he tried every day for the rest of his life. Eventually this pursuit consumed him, and he could do nothing else. When she perceived there was no love in her husband's heart for any but himself, the court lady pined away and died. Khasib never married again, and upon his demise, his kingdom passed to a lazy and foolish cousin."

Shahrazad fell silent. And the only sound that could be heard was the wind as it whispered its way across the sand to murmur among the branches of the date palms.

"Do you know that is the first time I have ever heard you finish a story?" asked Shahrayar.

It was a thing Shahrazad knew well, in fact, though she wasn't about to reveal this.

"So it is," she replied.

"And another thing," said Shahrayar. "Why is it that the kings and princes in the stories you tell are such great idiots while the women are so wise?"

At this, Shahrazad gave a chuckle. "Is it truly so? I had not noticed."

Shahrayar snorted. "It was a long story for such a small piece of cloth. It grows late. I suppose that we should go."

"Yes, I suppose we should," Shahrazad agreed. But for a moment, neither of them moved. Shahrayar lay with his head in Shahrazad's lap. No longer needing her fingers to read the cloth, she combed them through his hair. A great silence seemed to settle over them—as if they had been contained within a bell jar.

And in this silence, Shahrayar suddenly sat up and gathered Shahrazad into the circle of his arms.

"Who am I? I want to hear you say it."

And she answered, "Shahrayar."

At this, Shahrayar's heart gave a great leap, for she had not said that he was king. She had said his name, and that was all.

"Shahrazad," he whispered. "*Shahrazad!*" Then his lips found hers and neither spoke aloud at all.

The wind returned, and the scrap of cloth her mother had used to bind her wounds so long ago blew from Shahrazad's lap and went racing away across the sand. But neither she nor Shahrayar noticed.

When at last the kiss had ended, Shahrayar said, "Ah! Now I think I understand."

Shahrazad put her head upon his shoulder. "Understand what?"

"Why the kings and princes in your stories are such great idiots."

"And why is that?"

"Because everything about them is greater than that of other men. Another man would have kissed you long ago. He would not have waited so long to satisfy the longing in his heart."

At these words, Shahrazad's own heart began to pound like thunder. "And how long has your heart longed to kiss me?"

"Since the first day we were wed. How long has yours longed to kiss me?"

"Since that same day," Shahrazad acknowledged.

"I am glad to hear it," Shahrayar answered with a grin Shahrazad could hear in his voice. "For it makes you just as great an idiot as I am."

Shahrazad laughed. And so Shahrayar opened his mouth to ask one thing more:

Does this mean that you have come to love me, Shahrazad?

But the words were never spoken, for suddenly a nightbird called. At this, Shahrayar perceived how late it was. While Shahrazad had told her tale, time had seemed to hang like a great golden ball tossed high into the air. But now that she had finished, it swiftly came back down. The sun had already begun to slip below the horizon. Soon it would be dark, and in the darkness, dangerous things could lurk, even in a country such as Shahrayar's.

"Come," he said. "We must go. It is later than I thought."

So together they rose, and Shahrayar put Shahrazad before him on his horse just as before. But this time, she turned so that one of her arms was around his back, and so each held the other as they rode. Shahrazad fell asleep with the wind flowing over her like silk and her husband's heart beating against her ear like a brass gong.

And in this way they rode back to the palace as the night settled over them like a great dark cloak stitched with silver stars.

❧Eighteen❧

DINARZAD PULLS A THREAD

They returned to find the palace in pandemonium.

When night had fallen and her sister did not send for her, a thousand images of disaster had sprung up like wildfire in young Dinarzad's mind. Chief among them was the fear that King Shahrayar had heeded the whispered rumors that Shahrazad was practicing magic, and the only way to prove himself still a proper king was to put her to death after all.

Even in her agitation, Dinarzad knew better than to go to her father with her fears. Over and over again the vizier had counseled his youngest daughter to remain patient. To trust not only her sister, but also Shahrayar. But even though she had made her limbs obey, Dinarzad had found herself unable to follow her father's advice in the deepest reaches of her heart. For it seemed to her that as long as Shahrayar held Shahrazad's life within his hands, he was not some-one who was safe to trust.

So she did not go to her father with what she feared, and even if she had, she would not have found him. For he was still away upon the fool's errand Shahrayar had set for him that morning. And so it came about that Nur al-Din Hasan could not prevent what was to come.

Instead, Dinarzad poured her heart out to 'Ajib, the only person other than her father and sister she had come to trust. In the days since he had come to live in the vizier's household, he and Dinarzad had spent much time together, and she had come to love him well. For the vizier had not treated him like a servant, but rather like the son of an old friend.

At 'Ajib's suggestion, he and Dinarzad set off for the king's rooms, unsummoned. They did not know if they would be let in, for to go to the king's private quarters when he had not called for you himself was a thing unheard of. But Dinarzad's fear for her sister had now become so great that she was willing to risk whatever it took to make certain Shahrazad was safe from harm.

Through the corridors of the palace they walked together, their hearts beating fast—though each for a different cause. For courage, Dinarzad clasped 'Ajib by the hand. What he thought as he walked beside her, he never spoke aloud to another living soul, though this much I will caution you: Not merely by what happens next, but by all his actions may you judge him 'ere this tale is done.

And so at length, Dinarzad and 'Ajib came to the king's quarters and were admitted inside. For even though they had not been called for, none thought their appearance strange. Had they not been summoned for many nights now?

180

But when they came into the room and found it empty, it seemed to Dinarzad that her worst fears were realized. Unable to contain herself, she broke down. Her wild lamentations brought first the guards, and then the chamberlain dashing into the room.

When the chamberlain perceived the king was not where all had believed him to be, he raised the alarm. In a very few moments, all was as chaotic as a sandstorm. And in that maelstrom, only 'Ajib kept his head. He sent a message to his brothers of just one word, and that word was: "Now."

And then into the heart of this chaos came Shahrayar and Shahrazad.

At the sight of her sister, Dinarzad gave a great cry and launched herself into Shahrazad's arms. Shahrazad tried to soothe her to no avail. Dinarzad could not be calmed.

"Where were you? I came to find you, and you were not here! Where were you?" she sobbed.

"Hush, now!" Shahrazad pleaded. "You must calm yourself, little one." To her surprise, she found herself reluctant to tell her sister where she had gone. For the day was special—a treasure that belonged to Shahrazad and Shahrayar alone. "I was safe in the company of the king. I am back now. That is all you need to know."

"Safe?! How can you be with him and still be safe?" cried Dinarzad. "I know why you will not tell me. It's because you don't love me anymore!" For even in her anguish, Dinarzad sensed her sister was keeping something to herself, and it wounded both her heart and her pride.

"Oh, come now, that is nonsense," said Shahrayar. He moved to where the sisters clung together. "Your sister loves you well, Dinarzad. I am sorry if you feared for her safety. But I would never let any harm befall her. This you must know."

At these words, Dinarzad gave a wild laugh. She twisted in her sister's arms until she faced Shahrayar.

"No, I don't know that!" she cried. "How can I, when every day you hold the threat of death against her throat like a bright-edged sword? You can end her life whenever you wish. It is being married to you that puts her in harm's way."

"Dinarzad!" Shahrazad exclaimed, appalled.

At the shock and dismay she heard in her sister's voice, Dinarzad lost herself completely and spoke things that she should have kept locked close in her heart.

"I did what you asked of me. I did everything you asked," she sobbed. "I begged you not to do this, but you would not listen. Not to me, and not to Papa. Now you love the king better, and it is not fair! I wish I had never asked for a story at all. I helped you, and you betrayed me. It would have been better if you had died!"

At Dinarzad's words, a terrible silence fell. In it, all eyes turned to King Shahrayar. Though she could see none of this, Shahrazad understood at once, for she felt a hand as cold as ice close around her heart.

Now it comes, she thought. *He will look at me and see only deception, as I feared so long ago. I have tried, but I have failed. Now, we will both lose all.*

"What does your sister mean?" the king asked. "Explain her words to me, Shahrazad."

At the coldness in his voice, Dinarzad's tears froze upon her cheeks, and she realized the harm that she had caused. She made a strangled sound.

"Silence!" said Shahrayar. "I will hear from none save Shahrazad. Answer me. *What have you done?*"

And Shahrazad pulled in a breath and answered calmly. "That which I thought I must. No less. No more."

"That is no answer, and you know it!" exploded Shahrayar. "Always you speak in riddles. But you will answer me truly right this instant, or I swear before these others that I will slay you here and now."

In the silence that fell across the room, the only sound that could be heard were Dinarzad's heart-broken sobs.

"You do not speak, Shahrazad," Shahrayar said. "Can it be that you have nothing to tell me? Very well. Since you have no tale for me, I will tell you one:

"Once upon a time, a woman wed a king, though she knew that in so doing, she must die. But then she did a most clever thing: To save her life, she began to tell him a story that went on and on. In this she had the help of her sister. And also, I think, her father, for the family was always a close one.

"But now we come to the tale's great mystery," Shahrayar continued, his voice like the crack of a whip. "How long might such a tale have lasted, Shahrazad? Long enough for the woman to plot against her husband? To betray him and find another to sit upon his throne?"

"No," Shahrazad said. "No, Shahrayar." At her words, a single tear welled up from the split in her breaking heart. In silence, it rolled down her cheek.

"Do not think to move me with tears," said Shahrayar. "I am not so weak. Tears are the weapons of the desperate. I had thought better of you, Shahrazad."

"Think of me what you will," she said. "Indeed, I cannot stop you."

"Do you deny that you have done these things?" Shahrayar cried. "Did you not plan to so captivate me with your stories that I would long to spare your life?"

"I did," said Shahrazad.

And these two words brought Shahrayar such anguish he feared he would never recover from it. He would live with this pain all the days of his life.

"I will ask you this once, and then never again: *Why, Shahrazad?*"

At this, a second tear flowed down her cheek.

"Because I could see no other way. I needed time."

"Time for what?"

"To help you know your heart again," Shahrazad said. "And mine. For only then could all be made right."

Merciful heaven! thought Shahrayar. He could hardly have believed it possible that his pain could increase, but it did so now. How close he had come, that very day, to proclaiming that a thing was growing for her in his heart and that it might be love! And all because of a ruse, a trick. From start to finish, she had deceived him. There was nothing true in her at all.

"You should not dare," he said. At the sound of his voice, all within hearing felt the hair on the back of their necks stiffen and their limbs twitch as they fought back an instinct to run. "Don't dare to stand there and say you love me now. I am done playing your game. I see you for the deceiver you are. Take this woman away. I never want to look on her again."

"Where—" The chamberlain's voice came out in a squeak. He cleared his throat and tried again. "Where would you have us take her, my lord?"

And suddenly the king was weary—weary as he had never been before. For it seemed to him that now he faced the bleakest part of his vision. He was but one word away from spending the rest of his days without even the hope of love. For what hope would there be without Shahrazad?

But before he could proclaim where he would send her—nay, before his mind could even decide— a sound reached the ears of all in the chamber: swords clashing together, and voices crying out in alarm. Shahrayar drew his great curved scimitar, but even as he did so the doors to the chamber were hurled back and 'Ajib's four older brothers rushed into the room, followed by their most trusted soldiers. For many moments, the fighting was fierce as Shahrayar's guards sought to protect him. They fought bravely, but the unholy lights of greed and revenge burned in 'Ajib's brothers' eyes. They killed the chamberlain where he stood before the king. Then with a great cry of triumph, the eldest brother raised high his sword and struck at Shahrayar.

Shahrayar parried the blow. Their swords met with a great clang, and the shock of the blow nearly shattered Shahrayar's arm. He faltered back a step, then held his ground.

"See!" the eldest brother taunted. "See how he is hampered by his feelings for the sorceress, for he protects her even now. Truly, her power must be great!"

And in this way did Shahrayar realize that at the first sound of danger, he had leaped to protect Shahrazad. So perfectly did his body obey his heart in this that the action was concluded before his mind could realize what he had done.

"Let us see if she can save you!" the eldest brother said. Once more, he raised his sword. But as he brought it down, a figure suddenly darted forward.

"No!" it cried and thrust its head straight into Shahrayar's stomach, knocking him down. Instantly Shahrazad flung herself across him, and beside her was Dinarzad.

The eldest brother swore viciously when he saw what had been done. Much as he desired Shahrayar's death, he was not yet so far gone that he would make war on unarmed women. That would be the act of a coward. So he turned his sword on 'Ajib, the one who had foiled his attempt on the king.

"What do you think you're doing?" he bellowed.

"Leave him alone!" the second brother cried. "If not for him, we never would have come so far." And so they began to quarrel even in the midst of their triumph. But Shahrayar did not notice this. Instead, he made an anguished sound. The reason 'Ajib's face had stayed in his mind was suddenly clear. Viewed alongside his brothers, his resemblance to them was plain. Though each was different, they were still as alike as coins struck from the same mold.

"Ah!" Shahrayar said. "I see it now. I have harbored a snake."

"Truly," the second brother agreed with a sharp laugh. "A viper. But now that we are victorious, he need hide no longer."

He signaled the soldiers to move forward.

"Give up your sword," he said to Shahrayar, "or I will make your wife and her sister suffer for it, though I keep them alive."

"Shahrayar," Shahrazad cried in a low voice. Not because she feared for herself, but because she knew what he would do, even though he did not love her. Beside her, Dinarzad began to weep once more, and at the sound, 'Ajib turned his head toward her as if pulled by a cord.

"Dinarzad."

"Do not speak to me, traitor!" she sobbed. "For a snake speaks always with a forked tongue."

"I am waiting," the second brother said.

"So," said Shahrayar. He got to his feet, and the women fell back. Hilt first, Shahrayar presented his sword. No sooner had he done so than the second brother snatched it up and brought the hilt Shahrayar had presented down upon his head. The king dropped to the floor like a stone. At this, the soldiers seized the two women. Then the second brother knelt before the first and presented him with Shahrayar's sword.

"The palace is ours," he said. And then he grinned. "What do you command shall be done with the prisoners, my lord?"

The first brother reached with greedy fingers for Shahrayar's sword. "Let the *former* king be imprisoned in the darkest dungeon that may be found. No light. No air. No sound. Though he be alive, let him be put in such a place as will make him long for death."

"And the women?"

"Let the girl be kept fast in her own rooms. Take the sorceress to the highest tower. Perhaps she will find a way to admire the view."

So saying, the eldest brother laughed. And all that he had commanded to pass was made so.

❖ Nineteen ❖

IN WHICH 'AJIB LEARNS TO SEE
HIS HEART

And now began a time which, forever after, the people of that land called the Days Without Light. For though the sun shone as fiercely as ever, the light that had sprung from the teachings of Shahrayar's father seemed, with Shahrayar's imprisonment, to have been completely snuffed out. It was hidden away in a place of great darkness, just as Shahrayar was.

Now fear walked abroad in the land, for the new king's spies were everywhere, and a man could be deprived of all he held dear for no more than an unclean thought. Yet how a thought could be ascertained when it was never spoken aloud, none could tell. It was a thing known to the king's spies alone.

Soon friend was divided from friend, and neighbor from neighbor. Mother from daughter, wife from husband, father from son. No one knew who could be trusted anymore, and so they trusted none. And in this way, a great darkness covered all the land, for it came to dwell in every heart. And in this way did Shahrayar's people come to understand what it was to live beneath a tyrant's thumb.

Great barricades went up in and around the city.

For it seemed to the newly proclaimed king that it could not be long before Shazaman would come with an army to defend his brother and reclaim the throne. But the days passed, the tension increased, and still Shazaman did not come. Gradually the barricades fell into disrepair as the king and his brothers became complacent.

See! How easy it was to rid ourselves of this Shahrayar, they congratulated themselves. *We are so strong, none dare oppose us.* And so they stopped being vigilant, but the Days Without Light went on.

For now that nothing could contradict their will, the brothers' true natures were revealed—the new king's most of all. For it was soon seen that he was one who could only put on the outward raiment of a king. He did not possess the heart of one. His people mattered nothing to him. All that mattered was that he sat upon a throne.

Fights broke out within the city as the people daily grew more desperate and hungry. For here, unrecognized by the king and his brothers, the true battle was being waged by Shazaman.

Knowing that it would take time to raise an army to come to Shahrayar's aid, Shazaman had cut off supplies to the city at once. No caravans had arrived from Samarkand since the day Shahrayar had been deposed. In this, though it grieved his heart to know the people would suffer, Shazaman followed not only his own counsel, but that of Nur al-Din Hasan.

For the fool's errand Shahrayar had assigned to

his vizier had turned out to serve both well. The vizier was not within the palace when it fell. Hearing what had happened, he made for Samarkand at once to join forces with Shazaman. This his mind knew was the proper thing to do, though it cost his heart dearly, for he had to leave his daughters behind.

When he learned of the people's desperate condition, the new king posted soldiers around the royal granaries and storehouses so they might be secured for his use alone. In this way did the people learn that as long as the king himself ate well, he did not care if they starved. In fury and desperation, they dared to storm the palace itself. Their numbers were so great, they overcame the guards and streamed into the courtyard where once so many had gathered to see Shahrazad's execution and had learned instead that she would keep her life.

But life was not a thing those who came to the palace learned that day. It was a day to learn of death alone. For the king had his fiercest soldiers cut the people down until the stones of the courtyard ran with blood and were stained red from that day forward. At this, the riots ceased. None came to the palace, and the king and his brothers congratulated themselves yet again.

"See how the people fear and obey me," the new king cried. "Living under Shahrayar has made them weak and bold at the same time. They thought that they could challenge a king's authority. But I have proved them wrong!"

All it had taken was a firm hand. There would be no more uprisings.

Out of all the brothers, only 'Ajib had watched events unfold with horror in his heart. From her tower, Shahrazad heard the cries of the people and wept until she could weep no more. And in later years it was said that if one could find a place in that terrible courtyard that was not stained red, it would be a place where one of her tears fell.

But Shahrayar knew nothing of the massacre of his people, for he was kept imprisoned so deep within the bowels of the earth that he was completely in the dark and alone. Another man's will might have broken in such a place, but not the will of Shahrayar. Day and night, though he could no longer tell which was which, his will burned with its own light: the desire to win back his people and his throne. But even though he dared to dream of these things, he did not know how to dream of Shahrazad. And so, though his will burned bright, his heart still remained in the dark.

The days following the great massacre in the courtyard were the darkest days that land ever saw. On these days, or so it was said in later years, it seemed to many that the sun did not rise at all.

Then slowly a change began to occur so gradually as to be almost unnoticeable though it is surely there, like the flush that moves across the land when spring begins to come. More and more, 'Ajib went out into the city. Dressed in the clothing he had worn while working in the kitchens, no one paid him any mind. Sometimes he spoke, but mostly, he listened. And so he began to learn that in spite of all the evil being perpetrated upon them, the people were beginning to take heart once more.

Food was beginning to trickle back into the city. For such was the cleverness of the vizier and Shazaman: They had taken a great gamble, and they had won. Though their actions had first helped deprive the people of hope, they had also made it possible for the usurper to reveal the kind of king he truly was. Now that he had done so, there was room for hope to return with the help of Nur al-Din Hasan and Shazaman.

'Ajib's brothers might have believed the people had ceased to riot because they had been cowed. But 'Ajib knew that in this, his brothers were wrong. The people's bellies were beginning to be filled again with food supplied by Shazaman. But he claimed no credit for himself. Instead, every good deed accomplished by his will was done in the name of Shahrayar. With every mouthful of food they ate, the people's love for Shahrayar was rekindled, and they felt a longing for him to rule once more with Shahrazad at his side. For the way the kingdom had begun to prosper when she wed Shahrayar was a thing each bite of food brought to mind.

When 'Ajib realized what was happening, a horrible battle began to rage within his heart. Should he not tell his brothers what he knew? Surely they had first claim upon his loyalty, for they were his kinsmen, were they not?

But as he stared down at the palace courtyard, stained now and for all time with blood, 'Ajib felt his heart break apart and scatter like food for carrion birds. How could he tell his brothers what he knew when to do so would provoke the shedding of yet more blood? And there came into his mind thoughts which, once planted, could not be rooted out: His brother was no true king. In helping to place him upon the throne, 'Ajib had done a great wrong.

In that hour 'Ajib longed for Nur al-Din Hasan, for the vizier had always treated him kindly—not like a servant, but like a son. But he was far away in Samarkand with Shazaman. Kept away by the very acts that now brought 'Ajib such despair.

Finally, worn out and confused, 'Ajib made his way to his second brother's quarters. For he was the only one of his brothers in whom 'Ajib thought he might confide. But when he arrived there, he learned a bitter thing: His brothers were in conference without him.

And they plotted the death of Shahrayar.

"We must delay no longer," the third brother said. "Every day we allow this Shahrayar to live, he is a danger to us."

"We should have killed him at once," the eldest, now king, concurred. "I would have done it had 'Ajib not stopped me."

"Where is 'Ajib?" the fourth asked. "Why is he not here?"

"You know why he is not here," the second spoke up finally, and the sound of his voice was like an arrow in 'Ajib's heart. "He protected Shahrayar. We can trust him no longer."

And in this way did 'Ajib learn that his struggles over whether to betray his brothers had been for nothing. For they had betrayed him with no struggle at all. He stayed long enough to overhear the plans they made, the likes of which made his blood run cold. Then swiftly he returned to his quarters and wrapped Maju's trunk up in a cloak. For he had taken it and kept it safe, his brothers not recognizing it for what it was.

Then he took his swiftest horse from the stables, lashed the trunk behind him, and set out with all speed for Samarkand, spurring his horse on with need and hope.

❖Twenty❖

THE EYES OF THE HEART

*B*ut what, you wonder, in the Days Without Light, came to pass in the hearts of Shahrayar and Shahrazad? For they had parted in bitterness, in fear and in sorrow, their hearts still hidden each from the other. Yet the time was coming when all would depend on what their hearts might decide. Or, had perhaps decided already, but had not yet recognized.

The day after 'Ajib had left the city, great trumpets sounded, the palace gates opened, and the new king's herald went forth. Throughout the city he passed crying the king's will, and it was this: The lady Shahrazad was to undergo a trial. She was a sorceress, and so must lose her life. But if she could perform one good deed before her death, she might save the life of her husband, Shahrayar. In three days' time, the trial would take place. Once the sorceress no longer lived among them, peace and prosperity would flow into the land once more.

All through that day, and in the days that followed, the herald pronounced the king's will throughout the city, returning to the palace only at the sinking of the sun.

The day before the trial was to take place, the

second brother's curiosity got the better of him, and he made the climb to Shahrazad's tower. How had she taken the news that this time she must surely die?

"I would make peace with God, if I were you, Lady," he advised. "For it cannot be that you will live through tomorrow."

Though she had shed many tears over the fate of her husband, his people, and his kingdom, Shahrazad let no tears fall now. For the others, her tears were all spent. And she had promised herself before she wed Shahrayar that regardless of the outcome, never would she weep for herself.

"What I have to say to God is for His ears alone," Shahrazad replied. "I would look to your own soul, if I were you. It is your deeds that are black, not mine."

At this, the second brother became angry that he could not shake her composure, and he went back down.

Shahrazad did not sleep that night. Sometimes she paced back and forth upon her balcony so that she might feel the wind upon her face. Other times she sat by her brazier, still as stone. And in those hours, the darkest that had come to her since Maju died, Shahrazad waged her own battle: the one to see and understand her heart. For she did not want to leave the world without knowing herself. Did not want to perish knowing that she had been a coward while she lived. How could she face death unafraid if while she still breathed, she had feared to face herself?

In the still hour just before dawn, when all the

world holds its breath, fearing that this may be the day when the sun fails in its promise to return once more, Shahrazad grew so weary that she lay down upon the cold stones of the tower—just as Shahrayar had done before her not so very long ago. And as she did, she relinquished her struggle, just as he had relinquished his heart. And as she did, a thing happened that she did not expect, for she saw what her heart contained for the very first time. And what she saw was this: She loved Shahrayar—heart and body, mind and soul.

She did this knowing full well that he might not love her. For now she also understood a thing she had not before: The words the first queen had uttered before her death had been a curse indeed, for they had spoken only that Shahrayar must find a woman who could know his heart truly and be unafraid to have her own heart known. Nothing had she said of love. But with her words she had placed the fear of love over Shahrayar's head, even as she had kindled the desire for it in his heart. And in this she had shown that she knew her husband well. For he had come to fear nothing save the things she had planted within him: Not death or mischance, but betrayal and unrequited love.

When she understood this, Shahrazad understood the time of her destiny had truly come. So she got up and washed her face, tidied her garments as best she could, and went to stand once more upon the balcony, her blind eyes toward where the sun would come. For she did not doubt that it would reappear.

And so the second brother found her, will set, demeanor calm. And thus it was his heart that quailed as he led her down the long stairs to the great audience hall. His heart, not Shahrazad's. All the way, the second brother searched his mind to find the flaw in the plans that had been laid, but could discover none. But neither could he shake the feeling that with every step he took, events were slipping by him like the current of a river, moving faster and faster until they were beyond his control.

"Where do you take me?" asked Shahrazad.

"To the great audience hall," the second brother answered. And as he spoke, they arrived, the doors were thrown open, and they passed inside. Down the long length of the hall they walked, through a room thronged with as many people as had witnessed Shahrazad's marriage to Shahrayar.

Long had the brothers argued over this, but in the end, the king's will had won. For he wanted many eyes to see what was about to take place, to witness Shahrazad condemn herself and Shahrayar. In this way he hoped report might make him blameless in their deaths and proclaim this fact both far and wide. Both common people and courtiers had the king brought together so that all might perceive how great his power was.

"Let the prisoners be brought forth," he commanded when Shahrazad had been led in and made to kneel before his throne.

At this, a great gong sounded, and all those who had been imprisoned since the king had come to power were led forth, including Shahrayar. But he had been kept in so dark and terrible a place that none who looked upon the prisoners recognized Shahrayar for who he was. At the sight of those who had been imprisoned, a murmur swelled up from among the ranks of observers in the hall, for many of the prisoners stumbled, as if their limbs had lost the sense of movement. Matted, filthy hair hung down over their faces, masking their features. At the early morning light streaming into the hall, some cried out and covered their eyes. Much as they longed to see the sun, they could not do it. They had been kept in the dark too long.

The king waited until the prisoners had halted and the hall had grown silent before he spoke once more.

"Look well on what befalls all who would stand against me," he said. "Lest their fate be yours. Let the lady Shahrazad rise and stand before the prisoners."

At this, another murmur of wonder arose from the prisoners themselves, for none knew why they had been brought, let alone that their fate might involve Shahrazad. The mention of her name provoked such turmoil in Shahrayar's breast that he took his hands down from his face so that he might see her, though his eyes could hardly bear the light.

"Hear now the trial that you must face," the usurper told Shahrazad. "It has come to our ears that you are steeped in magic, and I will not suffer a sorceress to live among us. For your life, there can be no reprieve. Whatever follows, you must die. But I will give you a chance to do a great good before you breathe no more."

Here he paused. All knew this much already, except for the prisoners, who were hearing it for the very first time.

"If, neither by word nor touch nor any other sign, you can find your husband among these prisoners, I will spare his life, though he must live out the remainder of his days in exile."

At this, many assembled within the hall cried out in joy. But Shahrazad was not among them. *Liar!* she thought, for since coming into the chamber, she had discovered an amazing thing: Having learned to see her own heart truly, she could now see other men's as well. And so she saw the blackness of the usurper's heart and knew he would not keep his word.

I am like the water bearer's daughter, Shahrazad thought. And as she realized this, she almost laughed aloud. Had not the water bearer's daughter triumphed in the end, though she had faced an impossible trial? *I thought the story was for Shahrayar. But now I see that I was wrong. It was for me, that I might remember to have both purity of heart and strength of mind.*

"What say you, Lady?" the king asked. "Are you content to undergo this trial?"

"No, I am not content," Shahrazad answered. "For who can be content to undergo a tyrant's trial? But I will submit, for I greatly desire to spare my husband's life."

"You must find him first," the king reminded her. "Let us see what your blind eyes can do." And then he laughed, and the sound was cruel.

So Shahrazad began her trial. Three times she paced before the line of prisoners seeking to know what was in each man's heart. In this way she saw much that gave her hope. In only one heart did she find a thing that brought her grief. And so at last, her footsteps halted before the man who stood in the very center, the others stretching around beyond him in equal measure on both sides. Even so was Shahrayar still balanced between light and dark.

"This man is Shahrayar, my husband, and true king of this land," she said, and her voice was the only sound in the great hall. Tears began to stream down her face, unchecked.

"Let your second queen now break the curse the first laid upon you in bitterness and anger," she went on. "I have seen your heart, and I know it does not love me. But I will do what I must and so be unafraid to have my own heart known. Look upon me then, and see what my heart holds for you. Only then will the curse be broken."

At these words, Shahrayar began to tremble, a thing that caused him shame, for he did not yet see this for what it was: Hope, rising up. His heart, yearning to break free.

"I am afraid," he said in a voice for her ears only. "I am afraid to look, Shahrazad."

"And I am afraid to let you see," she answered, her voice low. "But if you don't, then she has won, and her brothers with her. Is that what you want? Remember the tale I told you when the sun shone upon us, and take heart."

At this, Shahrayar became more steady, for he thought he caught a glimpse of the direction that she was going.

"I will," he said. And he did a thing that only Shahrazad understood. He closed his eyes. For suddenly he remembered the way in which the water bearer's daughter had given herself over to the sea to find her treasure. Even so, he gave himself over to thoughts of Shahrazad. With his eyes closed, he could no longer see her as she stood before him. And so he looked to find her within himself.

A thousand images seemed to fill him, all of them dazzling. There was no deceit or darkness in her. She was filled with light. She could not have betrayed him as he had feared. And so realizing, Shahrayar suddenly perceived the thing that he had hidden from himself for so long: his heart. For it was from this place that all his beautiful visions came. It was no longer stone, but flesh and blood. And realizing this, he was no longer afraid to gaze into the heart of Shahrazad. He opened his eyes. Straight into her heart, he looked. And there he found himself. For he dwelt in her heart as she in his.

But even as joy filled him like clear water poured into a crystal flask, Shahrayar knew a great fear also. For he remembered Shahrazad's words. She had looked into his heart but not found love. And so he reached for her, taking her hands in his, not noticing the way the people all around them cried out.

"You think you have seen my heart, but that cannot be, for I have only just discovered what it holds. Look again, Shahrazad. Then tell me what you see."

And she looked, and answered, "Love."

At this, a great ray of sun burst into the hall and illuminated her face. Shahrazad cried out and covered her eyes. Suddenly realizing what had happened, Shahrayar gave a great shout and took her into his arms. Only then did he perceive that a great commotion raged all about them.

"Seize them!" the usurper was shouting from his throne. "They have broken rules of the trial! Neither by word nor touch could Shahrazad find out her husband. Let them be seized and put to death at once!"

But now a thing happened that none expected. Most of the rest of the prisoners cast off their filthy robes to reveal themselves ready for battle, for they were armed. Swiftly, they formed a protective circle around Shahrayar and Shahrazad.

"Not while I still live," one said.

And from the ranks of the observers in the hall a voice called out, "See! It is Shazaman!"

At this, a great cry of joy went up from the people, common folk and courtiers alike. For they perceived that Shazaman had come to his brother's aid at last, and if he prevailed, all might be free of the tyrant's yoke.

Still, things might have gone ill, for the hall was filled with many soldiers who were even now drawing their swords. But before blood could be shed, Shahrayar himself stepped forward.

"Hear me!" he said in a great ringing voice, and at the sound of it, the soldiers stayed their swords. "A great choice is in your hands," Shahrayar said. "By your deeds will the heart of our nation arise once more or fall.

"Think! Look into your hearts as I have looked into mine. Will you live in darkness or in light? For which you will have depends on what is in your hearts as much as what is in the heart of the one who sits upon the throne. But this, I think you know already. Choose swiftly, then, strike hard, and make every stroke count."

For a moment nothing happened, and it seemed to Shahrazad that the entire hall was filled with figures made of stone. Then two things happened, both at once. The leader of the soldiers stepped forward just as the usurper himself unsheathed his sword.

"The first one of you to make a move toward him in friendship, I will slay myself."

"No!"

At the sound of Shahrazad's voice, all turned to her in astonishment. The protective ring around her parted, and she moved to stand beside Shahrayar.

"Let no blood be shed," she entreated. "For I can see into the hearts of all here as well as I can see into my own. Therefore I say to the usurper: It will do no good to fight, for you can never win. The hearts of the people belong to King Shahrayar."

At this, a great shout went up: "Shahrayar! King Shahrayar!"

But the usurper was so far gone, no words of reason could reach him. "Brothers! To me!" he cried. Not one of them moved, for those loyal to Shazaman had them in their power. And so it was 'Ajib who stepped forward, all alone. It had been his voice that first proclaimed Shazaman's presence. It had been his plan that had smuggled Shazaman, the vizier, and those whom they most trusted into the palace to aid Shahrayar. For he had seen that a small force might prevail where a larger one would not.

"I am your brother," said 'Ajib. "Though I do not think you called to me. Hear now what I proclaim to all. I will serve you no longer. Instead I offer my sword to King Shahrayar. The true king and his heirs, now and forever will I serve, and may my deeds wash away the dishonor that has stained our house."

"Traitor!" the usurper shouted. But when he would have sprung upon 'Ajib, Shazaman stepped forward and struck him down, placing his naked sword across his throat.

"Say what you wish, and I shall make it happen," he told 'Ajib. "I will be your brother, if you wish his life."

"No, do not kill him," 'Ajib said. "For I think it will be worse for him if he stays alive. His own greed and jealousy will eat him up. But gladly will I take you for my brother, for these others I here disown."

"Then you must take me for a brother also," said Shahrayar. At this, 'Ajib knelt at Shahrayar's feet and wept, even as soldiers hauled his former brothers away.

"Forgive me!" he cried.

"There is nothing to forgive," Shahrayar said. "For it is already done. Come now, help to prepare our victory celebration. You know your way about the kitchens, I think?"

'Ajib laughed as he rose to his feet. "I do. But first let us see about a bath for you, my lord."

And in this way were Shahrayar and Shahrazad united in truest love and Shahrayar restored to his throne. And all without a single drop of blood being spilled upon that day, for of bloodshed there had been enough.

❧Twenty-one❧

ALL THE THREADS ARE WOVEN UP

And so it was that Shahrayar came into his own again, a better and wiser man and therefore a better and wiser ruler than he had been before. For through his ordeal and his own trial, he had come to see the secrets of his own heart and thereby learned the way to look into the hearts of others. And also through the love he bore to Shahrazad did he learn this, for had it not been her heart that had showed him how it might be done?

For six full days celebration banquets went on throughout the kingdom, but in the great city that surrounded Shahrayar's palace most of all. Each day new caravans arrived from Samarkand, laden with delicacies from both near and far. The best of these were distributed to the people, and the king grew daily in their love.

On the seventh night when all the revelry was done, Shahrayar gathered those he loved best and trusted most around him in his private quarters. And these were his brother, Shazaman; his vizier, Nur al-Din Hasan; and also Nur al-Din's youngest daughter, Dinarzad. It goes without saying that Shahrazad was there, for except when he attended to affairs of state, she was never far from her husband's side. Also present was young 'Ajib, and he stood close to Dinarzad. When Shahrayar noticed this, he regarded his vizier with raised eyebrows. Nur al-Din shrugged his shoulders, and Shahrayar smiled. And so were many things decided without words that would bring great happiness in years to come.

When all were assembled and at their ease, Shahrayar stood and beckoned Shahrazad to his side. "Hear now the will of your sovereign," he said. "Tomorrow morning will it be proclaimed throughout the land that the lady Shahrazad is no longer in peril of her life. For I will have no other wife but her to the end of my days. And therefore, I hope her life may be a long one!"

When the vizier heard this, he shed tears of joy, and so did Dinarzad. But Shahrazad did not weep, for she knew this already. Instead she regarded her husband with shining eyes. Eyes that could now see his countenance as well as his heart. For in fulfilling her destiny, the heavy cloak of blindness had fallen from her eyes.

Then 'Ajib stepped forward. "Lady, I bring you a gift," he said. "Though, it is hardly mine to give since it is already yours." At this, he moved to the window and drew aside his much travel-stained cloak to reveal Maju's ebony trunk.

"I hid this from my brothers on the night you were taken," he said. "For I think my heart knew even then that I had done a great wrong. Then I took it with me when I went to Samarkand, so that your father might know I was speaking the truth when I said I wished to help restore to you your freedom and Shahrayar to his throne."

"I thank you," Shahrazad said. And 'Ajib bowed so low his head touched the floor.

"And now there is only one matter unresolved," Shahrayar said.

"What is that?" asked Shahrazad.

"Why, the tale, of course," Shahrayar answered. "What becomes of the king? Does he ever find his son?"

"There is only one way to find out," said Shahrazad. "You know what must be done."

So while the others made themselves comfortable around the room, Shahrayar knelt before Maju's ebony trunk. He opened the lid, and lifted out the cloth. But when he brought it to Shahrazad, he got a surprise. For she handed it back to him, saying, "You now have the skill to finish this story yourself."

So Shahrayar sat cross-legged on the floor and ran the cloth between his hands. At first he felt nothing save the weave of the fabric. Then like one who has studied a foreign language with frustration only to have it all make sense in one quick flash, Shahrayar perceived the story so strongly, the characters within it seemed to move beneath his hands.

He saw the king in his prime, full of himself, set out to find the seer and thereby discover why it was he had no son. He heard again the seer's prophecy, 'If you see what you desire but claim it not, long will be your path and great your sorrow.' And he saw the way the king, secure in what he thought he knew, failed to heed this warning.

He saw him tumble down a mountainside and encounter a young man searching for a long-absent father. He saw him fly through the air, carried aloft by a stone. And many more adventures did the king encounter, all of them related by Shahrazad. Until at last Shahrayar reached the place where her telling of the tale had ended, and, in his own voice, he went on.

"The king was old. He had spent his days wandering the earth, looking for a way back home. Weary and discouraged beyond belief, he knelt before a pool to take a drink of water. There he saw his face reflected in its surface.

"*Who is that stranger?* he wondered. Then, with dismay, he realized it was his own face that he saw. And in that moment, it seemed to him that he had spent his best days in a futile endeavor, traveling so far from himself he could no longer recognize his own face when it was before him. In this way he had lost everything he loved and still not attained his heart's desire.

"If he could not recognize himself, how could he ever hope to see and know his son?

"At this, his despair was so great who knows what he might have done? But he was spared from making a choice. For unbeknownst to him, the pool he had come upon was sacred to the inhabitants of that place. None might drink there save by the will of the ruler alone.

"Before the king could so much as cry aloud his despair, he was seized, and without further ado, thrown into that country's darkest dungeon. Many days he resided there without light or sound. While he had knelt beside the pool, it had seemed to him his way could get no darker, but now he discovered that he had been wrong."

At this, Shahrayar paused and lifted his head to look at Shahrazad.

"What?" she asked. "You chose this tale, not I."

"Hah!" Shahrayar said. Then he returned to the story once more.

"After the king had been imprisoned for a period of time he had no way to measure, the door to his cell was thrown open and a second inhabitant tossed inside.

"'Alas, my friend,' the king said. 'I am sorry that you have come to such a dreadful place, though I admit I am glad to no longer be alone.'

"'I'm afraid I won't be very good company,' replied the other. And so by the sound of their voices, the two moved to sit beside each other in the dark. 'For I have wasted my days and am in great despair. Indeed, I no longer care whether I live or die.'

"'In this we are much alike,' the king said. 'For in these words could I describe myself. Tell me your trials, and I will tell you mine. And in this way, we may at least pass the time until we learn what will become of us.'

"And so his companion told of a lifelong search for a father he had never known. Before his birth had the father set out, not yet knowing his wife was with child. All through his youth the boy had waited for the father to return. At last, when he had come to manhood and none could oppose him, he followed the first wish of his heart and set out to learn what had become of the father he had never known.

"But in this, though his intentions were good, he had done a great wrong. For his father had been a king, and he himself had become one when he was grown. Yet he had abandoned his people for his quest, putting the wishes of his heart before their welfare.

"'Alas! Alas!' the king cried when the other's tale was done. 'Your tale is all too familiar, for I have spent my days searching for a son.'

"Now the king related how he had gone to the seer, so long ago. But when he spoke of this, his companion suddenly sat up straight and seized him by the arm.

"'But I know you!' he cried. 'Did you not tumble down this same seer's mountain only to be carried off by a stone?'

"'I did,' the king replied, astonished. 'I remember now. A young man broke my fall, and I was rude to him, a thing I have since regretted, for he probably saved my life. From that day forward, nothing went the way I hoped.'

"'I was that young man!' his companion replied. 'I have regretted my rudeness to you, also. But I was in such a hurry to reach the seer, I hardly paid attention to what I spoke. I hoped she might tell me what had become of my father. Instead, she spoke these words: "If you see what you desire but claim it not, long will be your path and great your sorrow." And she spoke true, for from that day to this one, nothing I have done has turned out right.'

"At this, the king was seized with wonder. For it seemed to him that he was beginning to understand and that against all odds and hope, the end of his quest was now in sight.

"'What was your mother's name?' asked the king.

"'My mother!' his companion echoed, astonished. 'Jauhara.'

"'So was my wife called. She gave me a daughter named Jallanar.'

"'My mother has a sister by that name!' the other cried, his astonishment growing. 'How can this be?'

"'In one way only,' the king replied. 'You are the son I have desired for so long, and I am your long-lost father. In our anger, foolishness, and pride we failed to see these things when we met before. Therefore, long have been our paths, and great have been both our sorrows. But embrace me now, and let us rejoice in the time that we have left.'

"'My father!' the son cried, for so he was. 'With all my heart I will do so.'

"As they embraced, there was a noise like thunder.

The ground beneath them shook, and the walls of their prison fell over onto their sides. Father and son sat blinking in the sunshine. When their eyes would work again, they discovered they were once more on top of the seer's mountain.

"'Well, that took you long enough,' the seer remarked as she beheld them. 'Come to think of it, I don't know when I've ever encountered two more foolish mortals. But you have found each other at last, and I suppose that must count for something. Go home now, together, and repair the damage done to your people, for you may have longer to make amends than you suppose.'

"So saying, she vanished before the king and prince could so much as say 'thank you.' And with her vanished the mountain. When they looked around them, the king and his son discovered they were outside the very city from which both had set out so long ago.

"Returning to the palace, they at once made themselves known to the queen. Great was her joy at the sudden reappearance of both her son and her husband! So great, she only took them to task for their foolishness for a month. After that she subsided, and not long after, all was put to rights. The king ruled wisely for many years, and after him, his son. Neither ever left home again, instead leaving the exploration of the wide world to others.

"But that is a different tale altogether."

And, with these words, Shahrayar fell silent, for

his tale was done. "So," he said after a moment, his eyes twinkling as he gazed at Shahrazad. "My tale was one of a king so foolish he almost lost everything for not being able to see what was right in front of him."

"You chose it," Shahrazad said. "Not I."

"So you have said before," Shahrayar replied. "And I notice that once again, it is the women who are most wise."

"It is important for even a tale of magic to ring true," Shahrazad said, her face solemn. Then, she smiled. At this, all within the chamber began to laugh, but Shahrayar laughed loudest of all.

"What shall become of this now?" he asked, holding up the cloth.

"Will it please you to give it to me?" said Shahrazad.

"Gladly," Shahrayar answered. And he rose and put it into her hands. At this, Shahrazad rose also. With one great motion, she unfurled the cloth, and all within the room cried out.

For now all could see the figures moving through it. The cloth was dark no longer, but spun of finest gold.

"Wait a moment!" Shahrayar cried. "That is not the king's story, it is ours!"

"Even so," said Shahrazad.

And that very night, they took the cloth and hung it in a place of honor behind Shahrayar's throne. There it stayed through all the days of his reign.

Those days were many, and throughout them, all prospered. Shahrayar and Shahrazad were happy together and raised a family of many fine daughters and sons.

Shazaman returned to Samarkand, and with him went 'Ajib, and some years later, Dinarzad. For she forgave 'Ajib his treachery even as she gave him her love. And so they were married. But Shazaman never took another wife, and upon his death, the rule of his great city passed to 'Ajib and Dinarzad. And I think their descendants are living there still.

Nur al-Din Hasan lived long enough to give his younger daughter in marriage, but soon thereafter, he died. Great was the sorrow throughout all the land at his passing, for he had been much loved. Shahrazad and Shahrayar erected a great tomb in his honor and placed Maju in it beside him along with her ebony trunk. So husband and wife were joined together in death as they had been in life. But the manner of telling stories in the way of the *drabardi* became lost, and now their skill lies mainly in the telling of fortunes.

When the day came that Shahrayar the king breathed no more, Shahrazad his wife took down the cloth of gold from behind his throne. She bathed his body with her tears, then wrapped the cloth of gold around him. Thus was he buried. And so, though the tales that Shahrazad had told to save her life were remembered, the tale of her own life was not. In time, not even her children remembered it, and the tale of

Shahrayar and Shahrazad was lost to all others and kept within her heart alone.

Now, you who have read what has here been told may remember or forget it as you will. The telling of it is over, for with these words "The Tale of the Storyteller's Daughter" at last is done.